"Newcomer Jed Power channels the tough-as-nails prose of Gold Medal greats Peter Rabe and Dan Marlowe." —Shamus and Derringer award-winning author Dave Zeltserman

Praise for *The Boss of Hampton Beach*
"Fans of Dennis Lehane will revel in the settings and atmosphere...an absorbing read...a hard-charging plot...Boston nitty-gritty." —Charles Kelly, author of *Gunshots In Another Room*, a biography of crime writer Dan Marlowe.

Jed Power

Hampton Beach Homicide

a Dan Marlowe Novel

Dark Jetty Publishing

Published by
Dark Jetty Publishing
4 Essex Center Drive #3906
Peabody, MA 01961

Cover Artist:
Brandon Swann

ISBN 978-0-9858617-3-5

Acknowledgements

The author would again like to thank his editor, Louisa Swann, for her skillful work and her knack for making the editorial process fun and educational.

Also thank you to my first reader, my wife, Candy Power. I know I tried your patience.

This Book Is Dedicated To My Beautiful Daughters,
Courtney and Jackie,
With Love.

Chapter 1

I WAS GOING TO DIE. I was as sure of it as if I were strapped into an electric chair. I'd just made a drink for one of the regulars at Hampton Beach's High Tide Restaurant and Saloon. I was heading his way when the rubber mat between my feet and the floor started feeling mushy. Suddenly, I was taking short jerky steps, like a baby just learning how to walk. By the time I reached the customer my heart beat so hard I wondered if he might actually see my shirt moving.

I set the drink on the bar, backed away, and leaned against the back counter for support. What the hell was happening? I couldn't really be dying, could I? I still had too much to do with my life—a family and a business to win back. No way I was checking out now. Maybe it was the acid I took all those years ago kicking in again. Or I was having a nervous breakdown or losing my mind.

Anything was better than outright dying. Much as I tried not to think about it, thoughts of dying raged through my mind, accelerating like gasoline thrown on a fire.

I tried to pull myself together with little luck. I went through the motions like a zombie. Popped beer caps, poured drafts, made drinks. My hands shook like I had the DT's when I took money or handed back change. I was drenched in sweat and my mouth was bone dry. I could have used one of the beers I was pouring. Or better yet, a few of them.

It seemed like everyone should be able to see what was happening to me, but no one said a word. At least not until Dianne, the owner, came behind the bar, moved in close and said, "Dan, are you all right?" The look of alarm I saw on her pretty face didn't help my heart rate any.

I tried to reassure her, and myself too, I guess, but that didn't work for either of us, especially when I heard my voice shaking like an old man's.

"Dan, go sit down. I'll take over."

I didn't argue, just pulled off my apron and handed it to her. Then I walked around the long mahogany bar into the restaurant section of the business. One hell of a long walk. Felt like every eye in the joint was on me. I found an empty booth in the back, slid in, and sat there waiting for the world to end.

Finally, everything slowed down a bit. I could make it home now; there was no way I was going to be able to finish my shift. Luckily, I'd walked to work this morning. I'd be home in a flash, sipping a cold brew.

I dragged myself out of the booth, told Dianne I was heading home, and left.

What seemed like an eternity later, I stumbled up the steps of my cottage, burst inside, yanked three Heinekens out of the fridge, and drank them — fast. After that I felt ok — exhausted, but ok. I finished the six-pack and slept.

⬬

I got that same about-to-die feeling one morning almost a year later when I found the back door at the High Tide open when it should've been locked.

I hesitated for a moment, swallowing back a sense of unease. I reached into my jeans pocket and fingered the pill bottle I always kept with me. Even though I opened up five mornings a week, there was still one person who was there much earlier than me — Shamrock Kelly.

Shamrock was the dishwasher and all-around handyman at the High Tide. He came in every morning around four and cleaned the place up, vacuuming rugs, cleaning the bathrooms, and emptying the trash. Then he'd lock up and leave, usually before I came in, returning later to wash dishes during either lunch or dinner, sometimes both shifts. But not always. Sometimes he stayed right through and I'd find him hard at work when I showed up in the morning. I'd probably find him inside now, working on a busted dishwasher or plugged-up toilet.

Of course, this being the beach, there was the off-chance I was dealing with a break-in.

I glanced back toward the street, suddenly wishing my walk had been longer. About ten in the morning on a gorgeous sunny day, sky filled with big cotton balls stuck on its bright blue backdrop. The temperature was comfortable, just like you'd expect in May on the New Hampshire seacoast.

Not too much was open before Memorial Day on the beach, except on weekends. So most of the fried dough stands, T-shirt shops and cheap jewelry stores I'd strolled past were either closed or still boarded up. Opposite the stores, on the other side of Ocean Boulevard, was a large asphalt parking area that ran half the length of the beach. It'd been almost empty when I walked by, a far cry from summer when you couldn't get a parking spot with a shotgun. Come summer, traffic would be bumper-to-bumper and the exhaust fumes strong enough to gag a skunk. Beyond the parking lot was the beach and then the ocean, reflecting sun so bright it hurt my eyes.

I hadn't passed another soul on my walk to work. Again, a lot different than in peak season when even a tackle for the New England Patriots had trouble making progress on the congested sidewalks. When I'd arrived at the Tide a few minutes ago, I'd stood out front for a bit just thinking and looking at the two-story wood structure. The building took up half the block between two lettered streets. There was a smattering of nautical knick-knacks hanging all over the front, everything from plastic seagulls to lobster traps to oars and anchors. The High Tide Restaurant & Saloon is a great beach business — a real beach landmark. I ought to know; I used to own it.

After admiring the front I'd moved around back to the service entrance. That's when I saw the door. I was alone, without even a few traffic noises to bolster my courage. Being alone didn't usually bother me — empty streets were a nice reprieve from the summer crowds. Not this time though. I stared at the crack between door and frame and clutched the pill bottle in my pocket.

I swallowed hard, my mouth drier than lint in a clothes dryer filter. I'd had more of the attacks — good old-fashioned panic attacks, according to the doc — but as time went on they seemed to have slowed down in frequency. It could've been worse. The doctor didn't have to tell me what had brought them on. I knew — cocaine. Even after all this time being clean.

I let go of my security blanket — a vial of prescribed Xanax tablets — and pulled my hand from my pocket. I lugged those pills around everywhere. One under the tongue and presto, end of attack. Between the pills and the Heineken I pretty much had this anxiety thing under control. Yeah, I know, people with anxiety disorders aren't supposed to drink. But people have to do what they have to do.

But I didn't need a pill or a Heineken yet. I reached out, tugged the heavy steel door open, stepped inside.

I was in a small back room with cases of empty beers stacked all around. In front of me a cement floor corridor led to the kitchen. There was enough sunlight coming from the open door behind me that I could see through the kitchen to the swinging doors on the far side. Nothing seemed out of the ordinary.

"Yo, Shamrock."

No response.

My heart started tap-dancing against my ribs. Looked like I'd have to go through the building and check everything out. I wiped my sweaty palms on my jeans, took a deep breath, and headed down the corridor.

Most breaks on the beach were pulled by young kids, but I wasn't taking any chances. As I passed through the kitchen I grabbed a heavy metal pot hanging from an overhead hook and brought it along for company. I scanned the fryolators and ovens on the right wall, looking for a more formidable weapon and found none. The speed table that took up half the room was a lost cause as well. I got a good grip on the pot's handle and pushed my way through the swinging doors into the dining room.

The High Tide's dining room is like a thousand other eating establishments you've seen—half booths, half tables. I walked quickly to the front of the room and scowled. The glass-and-metal door on the cigarette machine next to the hostess station was wide open. A pillowcase stuffed with packs of smokes lay on the red carpeted floor in front of the machine alongside the smashed padlock and metal money holder. I stalked over to the cigarette machine and gave the change holder a little kick.

Empty.

My heart kicked up another notch as a scrapping noise came from the vicinity of the bar. I tightened my grip on the pot. No sense just standing there; I'd have too much time to worry. Too much worry led to too much anxiety. Too much anxiety led to a panic attack. So I walked right by the shoulder-high wooden partition separating the dining room from the bar area, moved right up to the bar, and stood like a statue.

From here I had a good view of the entire room. If the restaurant was like a thousand other restaurants, the bar was like a thousand other bars. The mahogany bar itself ran almost the entire length of the room. It formed an L at the far wall, right in front of a large picture window that looked out onto Ocean Boulevard and the Atlantic beyond. Captain's chairs lined the front side of the bar and along the back wall hung a standard bar-length mirror behind an abundant stock of every kind of alcoholic beverage imaginable. Scattered about the room were various-sized tables with two to four chairs around each. A few booths lined one wall. A full-size red and gold jukebox sat in one corner.

I could see almost everything, including myself, in the back bar mirror. I looked ridiculous standing there with the pot in my hand. The only place I couldn't see was directly behind the bar. Not hard to figure out where someone would be hiding. But I wasn't ready to go back there. Although I was still pretty sure I was dealing with kids, I wasn't that sure. So I stood there for a couple of minutes, straining to hear, until I finally got tired. I had to do something.

"All right," I said in the most threatening voice I could muster. "Come on. Get the hell out from behind there. Now." Nothing. I tried another tack. "I called the cops. You know how long it'll take them to get here. They'll bring a dog."

I didn't really know about the dog bit, but it did the trick. A head poked up behind the bar, near the bank of draft beer spigots. The Hampton Beach police station was literally one minute away, so I guess he didn't like the thought of one of their shepherds gnawing on his leg like a leftover bone.

"Let's go. Get over here," I said, my tension easing now that I could see the thief was just a young kid.

The boy walked around the far end of the bar and stood about thirty feet away, facing me. He was very young, around thirteen, maybe. I couldn't be sure. He had long blonde hair, long enough so that he had to keep flicking his head to keep the hair out of his eyes. He was tall for his age and thin, wearing a *No Fear* T-shirt and baggy shorts that ended below his knees. His sneakers were heavily worn and under his arm he was clutching a skateboard.

He looked just like dozens of other kids you see on the beach, especially in the off-season when the rents are cheap and you get a less prosperous group of people than the summer tourists who can afford to shell out the high weekly rents. I pegged this kid right away as one of these winter people. In a few weeks he wouldn't even be on the beach. He and his family would have to pack up and leave their motel room or cottage and make way for the big-money summer crowd.

We stood there staring at each other for a minute, me trying to decide how to play it with this young kid, him probably waiting for my move. He looked awfully uncomfortable.

"Well, do you have anything to say for yourself?" I finally said. He didn't answer, just lowered his head and tucked the skateboard in closer to his side.

"What's your name?"

He answered this time but so softly I couldn't make it out. "What did you say?"

"Kelsey."

"Kelsey what?"

"Sweeney."

I probably should have played the tough guy; I easily could have, anybody could have. He was a real beanpole — a stiff ocean breeze would have knocked him over. But as I watched him standing there in those big baggy clothes, looking down at the floor, feet constantly moving, I didn't have the heart. Besides, what good would it have done?

"Well, Kelsey Sweeney, you got yourself in a real jam here. What do you think I should do with you?"

I didn't expect the answer he floated back at me. "Call the cops, I guess."

Sure, that was my obvious option. It would have been the easiest thing to do: call the cops, they take the kid away, Shamrock cleans up the mess, the cigarette machine company gives us a new machine. End of story.

But then I started thinking of my own son, a son I didn't see much of anymore, and that how maybe someday my son could be standing where this kid was standing now and some other guy would be standing in my place.

"You ever do anything like this before, Kelsey?"

"No." Finally the kid said something I'd expected, even though I had no idea if it was the truth. Only one way to find out.

"Where do you live?"

The address he gave was a five-minute walk from the High Tide. "All right. Let's take a trip down there."

Kelsey Sweeney took two awkward steps toward me. His pants jingled and he grabbed them just before they slid off his skinny hips.

"On the bar," I said.

He held his pants up with his left hand, the skateboard tucked tight against his side. He started shoveling quarters out of his pocket with his other hand, dumping the change on the bar. When he emptied that pocket, he moved the board to his other arm and repeated the process, digging quarters out of his other pocket. I hadn't known a cigarette machine could hold that many quarters. When he was done, I jerked my head and said, "Let's go."

When he got near me, I snagged the skateboard, not because I was worried about being clobbered, but there was no way I'd be able to outrun the kid if he jumped on his board and took off. "I'll take that."

I walked him through the dining room, hanging the big pot on its hook as we passed through the kitchen and out the back door.

"Will your parents be home?" I asked.

"There's just Ma," he answered.

"We'll talk to her then."

"I hope she's okay." He lowered his head, the blonde hair covering his face.

I knew enough about winter people, about the substance abuse and worse, that I didn't have to ask any questions.

I fingered the pill bottle in my jeans pocket as we headed in the direction of Kelsey Sweeney's home.

Chapter 2

I WAS RIGHT—it took us about five minutes to reach Kelsey's neighborhood. It wasn't much to look at, although I'd expected that from the address he'd given me. His place was off Ashworth Avenue. Ashworth runs parallel to Ocean Boulevard almost the entire length of the main beach. They're both one-way streets, running in opposite directions with Ashworth traffic going south, and are connected by alternating one-way lettered streets. Anyway, the street we were looking for was one of the back streets off Ashworth, a dead end at the beginning of a large marsh, deep in what the locals called "out back." The whole street was an eyesore with dilapidated one- and two-family wood cottages on both sides. Rubbish barrels overflowed, most of them filled with liquor and beer bottles. A couple of mangy mutts circled around us as we headed down the street, more interested in me than Kelsey. I tightened my grip on the skateboard.

His home was halfway down on the right. The cottage was as old as all the others and had what looked like the original multi-colored asphalt shingles covering the sides. I followed him up the few stairs, not daring to touch the rickety railing, and was careful where I put my feet—the steps didn't look solid. The narrow porch had a few cheap white plastic chairs scattered about.

He opened the door, stepped in and called, "Ma?"

I went in right after him. The cottage looked the same inside as it did outside, like a hundred other cottages on the beach that the landlords had long ago stopped giving a shit about keeping up. At least it was clean. We wound our way between a couple of easy chairs in the tiny living room. I tried not to stare at the stuffing popping out of the chairs, a couch in not much better shape, and the scarred coffee table. There was a small TV sitting on what looked like an old end table in the corner. I wondered if the TV worked. The floor looked like linoleum that may have been white at one time. I set the skateboard down.

"Ma. This man wants to talk to you." Kelsey stood in a doorway, blocking my view of the next room. I came up behind him and gave him a nudge. He walked into the room and now I could see it was a kitchen. Curtains on the one window blocked most of the light, but I could still make out most of the details—the requisite sink, cabinets with chipped paint, a very small fridge that made a distracting noise, and a tiny kitchen table with two chairs. 'Ma' sat at the end of the table, facing me. She had long, stringy gray hair and was wearing a red plaid lumberjack coat, unusual for May. I couldn't tell how old she was but her face had an awful lot of living on it. We looked at each other. She didn't blink; I did. The glass on the table in front of her was almost empty, the ice cubes still big.

She didn't say a word, so I spoke up.

"We have a little problem here, Mrs. Sweeney." She still didn't say anything and I wondered for a moment if she was drunk. I see enough drunks in my line of work that I can usually tell; with her I couldn't. "I said..."

"Name's Cora and I heard what you said the first time. You don't have to say it again. I ain't deaf." She looked at the boy, who was standing there shuffling his feet and looking mighty uncomfortable. "So what's this problem, Mr...?"

"It's Dan. Dan Marlowe. I caught your son here inside the High Tide Restaurant. He broke in and smashed open the cigarette machine. He had more quarters on him than the owner of the Funland Arcade."

She didn't seem surprised. In fact, she didn't show any emotion at all. "Sit down, Mr. Marlowe."

I took the chair at the other end of the table. She took a Marlboro out of a pack and offered me one. I declined and she lit hers.

"Drink? Beer? Water?"

I shook my head.

"Well, I think I'm gonna need one." She spun around — I hadn't noticed that the woman was in a wheelchair — and propelled the big wheels with her hands, rolling across the floor to the fridge. She opened the door, grabbed some ice cubes, and rolled over to the counter on the other side of the small room. Kelsey jumped aside to get out of her way. She made her drink and rolled back to the table.

She looked at the boy again, then at me. Kelsey shifted from foot to foot like he wished he were somewhere — anywhere — else. I was starting to feel that way myself. I had a job to get back to and this woman didn't seem like she was in any hurry to end my visit. I snuck a look at the wheelchair — one of those old, clunky things — and wondered how long she'd been confined to it. And how had she gotten there in the first place?

"Come here," Cora said to her son. "Now."

He shuffled over to her. I winced, figuring he was probably going to get a good smack upside the head. I figured wrong. The woman put her arm around his skinny waist and pulled him right up tight against her and the wheelchair. Kelsey bent over and hugged her head in his arms. And it was natural, like they did it all the time. After a moment he stood up straight again, smiling for the first time since I'd met him. The woman still held his waist tight.

So that's how she was going to play it: them against me. But I'd read her wrong again. She spoke, her tone strict. "You do what this man says, Kelsey?"

He didn't answer.

"Kelsey?"

"Yes, Ma, but..."

"No buts. You break into someone's business and smash their property and all you got to say is 'but'? There's no 'but' with that kinda thing. It's wrong. You know that. I've taught you. This man could've called the police on you and he didn't." She glanced at me. "Did you?"

I shook my head.

"Now you get in your room. I want to talk to Mr. Marlowe myself. And you're going to be in that room for a long time so you better get used to it." She gave the boy a gentle shove toward another door. He looked happy to be out of there. I could relate to that.

When he was out of the room, Cora Sweeney took a sip of her drink and shook her head. "I'm sorry for what my son's done, Mr. Marlowe. Maybe all parents say it, but believe me, Kelsey's a good boy. And thank God I've got him. He's my strong right arm. All I've got. Without him, I don't know what I'd do." She patted the wheel of her chair. "I'm not looking for sympathy, but it's not easy here, like this. Especially in the winter. You know what the winters are like on the beach, Mr. Marlowe?"

I nodded. Winters were dark, desolate, and depressing here on the beach. And that was if you had two good legs and a car to get away in occasionally. In her situation I couldn't imagine how unpleasant those winters would be.

"It's just me and the boy. Has been for a long time now. Ever since I ended up in this damn thing and his father took off. I try to be a good mother, but it's hard to keep an eye on him all the time. There's a lot of temptations on the beach for kids. And besides, I've had some...differences with people around here, so I don't want him running around all the time anyhow. I guess all I can do is keep trying and pray."

There was a little catch in her voice and for an instant I thought she was going to cry. She didn't. Instead, she sat up straight in her chair. "Again, I'm sorry for what the boy's done. And he'll be punished, believe me. I don't want him getting away with things like that. If he did, I'd be scared where it could end."

Suddenly what the kid had done at the restaurant didn't seem so important. These people had enough problems; I didn't feel like adding any more. "It's not that big a deal."

"Yes, it is, and I want to thank you for bringing him to me instead of the police."

"That's okay." I was thankful now that I'd followed my gut instead of my head.

"There's damages," Cora Sweeney continued. "You said a busted cigarette machine. And he must've broken somethin' to get into your place."

"It's not my place. I'm the bartender. And there's insurance..."

She cut me off. "Insurance won't cover it all." She rolled her chair across the room and slid open a counter drawer. She came back to the table and pulled a big roll of bills out of the black plastic purse she'd just retrieved. "I have to keep a bit of cash around because I can't get to the bank very often."

I shook my head. I wasn't about to take money from a woman in a wheelchair living in a hovel out by the marsh at Hampton Beach. "Insurance'll probably cover all of it," I lied. "Why don't we wait and see? If it doesn't, I'll let you know."

She looked satisfied with that idea and snapped the purse shut. "All right, Mr. Marlowe. And believe me— if any money is due, the boy will be paying me back. I want to thank you again for bringing Kelsey to me and not the police."

I stood up, shook her thin hand, and left the cottage.

Walking back to the High Tide, I thought about Kelsey Sweeney and his mother and wondered how many other people were living on the beach in ramshackle, barely-winterized cottages. I knew it was plenty. After all, I'd been on the beach for a long time and I'd seen lots of people down on their luck like the Sweeneys. Usually in the off-season, shuffling past me on the street. I'd rarely been invited into their homes. And hadn't really understood what their lives were like.

Most summer tourists never saw winter people. A majority of those folks who suffered through winter were long gone before the vacationers showed up. Thrown out of their cottages and rooms before the summer season started. Vacationers could afford big bucks per week for a place on the beach; people like the Sweeneys couldn't. But the winter people always came back after Labor Day, in September, when the rents plummeted. The winter people got the most time at the beach, but they didn't get the best time. And I guess that's probably why you never saw one with a tan.

Chapter 3

THE DAY AFTER the break-in and my talk with Cora Sweeney, I was making banks for the lunch waitresses, counting change and bills out from the register behind the bar and placing it in individual coffee cups, and feeling more than a little guilty. I hadn't told Dianne I'd found anyone around when I'd discovered the break. The cops did some dusting (lot of good that'd do with thirteen-year-old fingers) and took a few notes, then said they'd follow up on it, which meant the investigation would go nowhere. Everyone assumed the thief had been spooked by something and left the smokes and change behind.

I tucked the filled coffee cups under the bar, grabbed a big green plastic bucket, and headed for the ice machine in the back room. As I came around the bar, I glanced at the new cigarette machine near the door. The place looked like nothing had happened. Shamrock had cleaned up the mess, but I knew from experience the insurance would stick Dianne with a deductible. As I scooped ice into the bucket on the first of five or six trips needed to fill the sinks at each end of the bar, I promised myself that I'd work payment for that deductible into the till as soon as I had a chance. I figured it was the least I could do for the down-on-their-luck Sweeneys. And for Dianne too.

After all, I owed both her and Shamrock an awful lot. It hadn't been so long ago that I'd stared into this very same ice machine and seen Shamrock's frozen face staring back at me. I'd been able to pull him out alive, barely. But I hadn't been able to forget how both he and Dianne had almost been killed trying to help me out of some trouble I'd gotten mixed up in, trouble involving cocaine smugglers, crooked cops, and drug dealers. I shook my head to get the image of Shamrock's frost-covered face out of my mind.

When I'd finished with the ice, I filled the rest of the sinks with hot water for washing glasses, restocked the beer chest from the large walk-in cooler out beside the ice machine, and turned on the two overhead TV's at each end of the bar. Then I attacked the fruits. With quick movements and a sharp knife, I sliced up oranges, limes, and lemons and dumped those, along with olives and cherries, into two trays, one for each end of the bar.

When I was ready for business I unlocked the front door. No customers yet, so I proceeded to do what all efficient day bartenders do—read the morning newspapers.

I grabbed my *Boston Herald* (I read that and the *Boston Globe* most days) and spread the paper on the bar in front of me. The front of the bar—where I was currently standing—faced the front of the restaurant, just a few feet from the large window that looked out onto Hampton's main drag: Ocean Boulevard. Beyond the boulevard sat the parking lot, beach, and Atlantic Ocean. A few cars and people passed by, but still it was a May tempo—more activity than most months but nothing like July and August. I liked it that way too, without the desolation of winter or the madness and heat of summer.

I was just getting into an article about a male Hollywood star caught with a transvestite hooker when a voice interrupted me.

"Ahhh, for the love a Jaysus, Danny. You're always readin' the paper. What's the number?"

I turned my head and there was Shamrock Kelly, High Tide dishwasher and all-around handyman. He was medium height, dressed in restaurant whites, and looked as Irish as a shillelagh. Shamrock and I go way back; he used to work for me when I owned the Tide. He stayed on when Dianne bought it, just like I did. And we've shared an adventure or two. I thumbed through a few pages and gave him the lottery number.

"Figures. I never win a thing."

"Maybe someday, Shamrock."

Shamrock shook his big head. "I dunno. The Luck o' the Irish skipped me, I think."

"That's not what they say around the beach."

"Ha, ha, Danny boy. Very humorous. Think we'll be busy today?"

"This is the restaurant business. If I could predict that, I'd be a millionaire."

"No matter. I'm gettin' paid anyway." Shamrock turned and headed in the direction of the kitchen. But before he'd gone more than two steps, he stopped and said, "Danny. Why didn't the chicken wear underpants?"

"Why?"

"Cause his pecker's on his head."

"Cute, Shamrock. Very cute."

The Irishman laughed loudly and disappeared into the kitchen. I returned to my newspaper and waited for my first customer.

I'd read all about the star and the transvestite hooker when I heard the front door swing open. I looked up as Kelsey Sweeney walked into the bar. I almost said something about returning to the scene of the crime, but pulled up short. Something was wrong. He was dressed in the same clothes as the previous day: T-shirt and baggy shorts. He even had his skateboard tucked under his arm, but his face was paler than a tourist from Canada. He glanced nervously around and when he saw me he came right up to the bar.

"What's wrong, Kelsey?"

His soft voice shook. "It's Ma. Something's wrong with her. I can't wake her up. Can you come down and look at her? Please?"

I reached for the phone under the bar. "You should've called 911."

"No, please, don't."

For a second I thought he was going to make a grab for my arm. Instead, he turned red and said, "Sometimes it's awful hard to wake Ma up. And she said to never call the police again if that happened because they might take me away from her."

I forgot the phone and came around the bar. "I take it this isn't the first time something like this has happened."

"No, sir."

I waited, but he evidently didn't have anything else to say. I put my hand on the boy's shoulder and herded him toward the front door. Before we left, I asked one of the waitresses who was setting up her station in the dining room, a waitress who also knew how to make drinks, if she'd watch the bar for a short while. She said she would.

Kelsey and I were barely out the front door when he slammed his skateboard down on the pavement, hopped on, and rolled down the sidewalk. I followed him to the corner where we turned and headed towards Ashworth. I could tell he was fighting to keep from going faster so I could keep up with him. I stepped up my pace and we were at his cottage in no time.

In one smooth movement he jumped off the board, stepped on the tail, and caught the board in his hand as it flipped into the air. I followed him up onto the porch, through the run-down living room, and into the kitchen. Kelsey stood in the kitchen doorway; I brushed past him.

Cora Sweeney was in the same spot I had seen her in yesterday. Except now she was face down on the kitchen table. Her arms hung limply over the sides of her wheelchair. I walked over and lifted her head. It was heavy — dead heavy — and I needed both hands. I took one look at Cora Sweeney's face, then set her head down gently and brushed the gray hair back from her bloodless cheek. Kelsey's mother had taken her last drink.

I glanced at Kelsey behind me. He looked almost as bad as his mom, but at least he was breathing. I reached for the black phone on the kitchen table and dialed 911. I told them there was an emergency and gave the address. I put the phone back in its cradle and turned around.

The boy was gone.

I ran through the cottage and out onto the front porch just in time to see Kelsey Sweeney riding low and fast on his skateboard. Before I could shout, he'd disappeared around the end of the street and onto Ashworth Avenue.

Looked like I'd been elected to stay and wait for the EMTs.

Chapter 4

IT WOULDN'T TAKE LONG for the EMTs to arrive. The fire station was right around the corner on Ashworth. So I walked back into the kitchen and took another look at Cora Sweeney. She looked kind of peaceful—her head resting on the table, her hair spread out like a gray curtain. An almost-empty bottle of Jack Daniel's sat at the edge of the table along with an overturned glass that had held the amber liquid.

I spotted something that I'd missed before protruding out from under her hair, so I gingerly lifted a clump of gray and found an empty prescription bottle for Xanax, a tranquilizer I was familiar with. I noticed a few of the tablets scattered about. I noted the pharmacy and the doctor's name, but let her hair fall back in place without touching the bottle.

A siren wailed close outside, so I walked back through the front room, stepping out onto the porch just as a red Hampton rescue truck pulled up. Two men in blue jumped out, one carrying a large emergency kit. I led them back to the kitchen, then got out of their way. I stood in the doorway, watching them do their thing. By the look on their faces I'd been right about Cora Sweeney's condition. She'd seen her last Hampton Beach winter.

The EMTs had only been working for a minute or two when I heard more sirens and other vehicles pull up out front. Feet clomped up the front steps and the door banged open. I turned to see Steve Moore, a Hampton police detective, come through the front room. He was probably in his late thirties, had a brown buzz cut, and stood about six feet tall with a healthy amount of weight, mostly muscle, packed on his frame. He wore a short-sleeve shirt and tie with a gun holstered on his hip, and was stuffing a pair of sunglasses into his shirt pocket as he approached. Steve was one of the few men on the beach who wore a tie—if you didn't count the Chamber of Commerce guy and real estate agents. Not only did I know him, he knew me. After all, cop and bartender were two of the most visible occupations on the beach. Everyone knows who you are. Most of the time that's a good thing, sometimes not so good.

"What the hell are you doing here, Dan?" Steve asked, staring past me into the kitchen. Before I could answer he popped another question. "You find the body?"

I nodded.

"Okay, sit down. I'll want to talk to you in a minute." Steve disappeared into the kitchen and I took a seat on the ratty couch that looked as old as the cottage itself. Firemen and uniformed cops tramped in and out but I hardly noticed. I wasn't looking forward to the questions Steve would be asking. I rested my hand on the prescription bottle in my jeans pocket, comforted by the feel of hard plastic pressing against my palm. I thought about Kelsey. Where the hell was he right now? What would happen to the poor kid now that his mom wasn't in the picture?

Steve came back into the room and sat on a worn chair across from me. He held a small notebook and pen in his hands. "All right, Dan. Let's start with what you were doing down here."

I fidgeted a bit in my seat. "Well, her son," I nodded toward the kitchen, "came into the Tide this morning and asked me to come down here. He knew something was wrong with his mom."

Steve clicked the pen a few times as he spoke. "Why go all the way up there to get you? Why didn't he just call 911?"

"He was scared, Steve. His mother had told him never to call the cops. I guess this wasn't the first time he'd found her passed out, but she'd always eventually woken up before. She was worried they'd take the kid away from her."

Steve looked up from the notebook he'd been scribbling in. "I get the scared part, but why you?"

Now I was really in a spot. I didn't want to get Kelsey in trouble for the break-in at the High Tide; he already had plenty to deal with. Plus, I'd never mentioned to Dianne or to the police that I'd found the person responsible for the break. I didn't want to lie, but I didn't have to give answers to questions I hadn't been asked. "He said he didn't know who else to get."

"How long have you known...what're their names anyway?"

"Cora and Kelsey Sweeney. And I haven't known them long."

Steve wrote some more in his notebook. "And you called 911 as soon as you got here?"

I nodded. "I saw her, could tell she was dead, and called right away."

"Didn't touch anything?"

EMTs, uniformed cops, and firemen kept up a constant stream coming and going from the kitchen. One of the uniformed cops stopped and spoke to Steve in a low voice.

I waited until the other cop walked away. "No, I didn't touch a thing except the phone."

"What did you see when you got here?"

"Exactly what you see now. Her head was on the table with the booze bottle and the glass." I didn't mention the prescription vial.

"So where's the kid?"

"As soon as he realized I couldn't help his mother he took off like a shot. I called 911 and then ran outside just as he was rounding the corner on Ashworth."

"Why would he do that?"

"Frightened, probably. Hell, he's just a kid. He probably figured someone would take him away like his mom warned him about. She must've had a real bad drinking problem."

Steve closed his notebook and put the pen in his shirt pocket. "That's an understatement." He looked toward the kitchen.

"So that's what it was? The booze?"

He shrugged. "And pills maybe. We found a prescription bottle, too. Probably got drunk, forgot how many pills she'd taken, and swallowed a few too many. Coroner will tell us for sure. It might even be she just bailed out."

"Suicide?"

"Don't tell me that shocks you. Was she year-round or winter?"

"I don't know."

"Either way, you know what the beach is like in the winter. I can't imagine what it'd be like stuck out here in a wheelchair to boot."

"Yeah, but this isn't winter."

"Doesn't matter. It could've built up. Maybe she couldn't take the thought of another one. Even summers must be rough down here in a chair like that, never going anywhere.

Anyway, they'll let us know what the cause was." Steve stood and stuck out his hand. "Good seeing you again, Dan, though the circumstances could've been better. You might as well get back to the restaurant. I might want to talk to you again though."

Jesus, the restaurant. I'd been gone longer than I'd expected. I wiped my hands against my jeans but didn't stand up—there were a couple of things still bothering me. "She... Cora...told me that she was having difficulties with some people on the beach."

Steve pulled back his hand and sat back in his chair. "With who?"

I shook my head. "She didn't say."

"What kind of difficulties?"

"She didn't say that either."

Steve shrugged and got up again. "I'll keep it in mind, but I wouldn't worry about it too much. Half the people on the beach don't get along with the other half. It's a little Peyton Place. They'd kill over a parking spot, for Chrissake. Although in her case, I guess we can rule that motive out."

"She also kept a roll in a black purse in the kitchen drawer."

"Okay, I'll check it out."

I finally stood up and asked the question that kept burning in my brain. "What about the boy?"

"Oh, don't worry. Is that him?" Steve pointed to a picture on the far wall I hadn't noticed before.

It was Kelsey all right. Long blonde hair plastered down, a forced smile on his face. I nodded.

"It's a small beach," Steve said. "We'll find him fast."

He moved back into the kitchen and I walked out of the cottage, down the porch steps, around the police cars, and up the street to Ashworth.

No matter what Steve Moore said, I was still worried about Kelsey Sweeney and what would happen to him.

Chapter 5

A DAY LATER I was walking home after work, lost in thoughts about Cora and Kelsey Sweeney and Steve Moore, when I suddenly heard the clackety-clack of a skateboard behind me. For a moment I thought it was my own son but that couldn't be. I couldn't remember the last time I'd watched and listened to him fly up the boardwalk on his skateboard. Still, maybe...I turned in time to see Kelsey Sweeney jump off his board, step on its tail, and catch the board with his right hand as it popped up. He tucked the board under his arm and fell into step beside me without saying a word. He looked the same as he had yesterday — same loose T-shirt, same baggy shorts, same long blonde hair he kept flicking out of his eyes.

I glanced around, half-expecting Steve Moore to pull up in his unmarked car. Although there was a little traffic, there was no sign of police cars, marked or un-marked. That wouldn't last long. The patrol beat consisted of heading south on Ashworth Avenue and then swinging around and heading north on Ocean Boulevard, then around again. For a little variety, sometimes the cops would shorten the loop by cutting through on one of the alternating one-way streets connecting Ashworth and Ocean Boulevard. So I knew a cruiser could come by any minute.

I put my arm around Kelsey's shoulder and led him off Ocean and down M Street. His thin body shook under my arm and when we were pretty well out of sight of traffic passing on the main drag, I stopped. "Kelsey, do you know the police are looking for you?"

"I know. They've chased me twice." He talked fast and kept chewing his lower lip.

I tried to reassure him. "They're not chasing you. They just want to talk to you about...your mother. I'm sorry, Kelsey."

And that's when he lost it. He started bawling and I put my arms around him just like I would my own boy. I let him cry like that for a while. There wasn't much foot traffic on this side street, and the few people who did pass by probably thought they were seeing a father comforting his son. After a few minutes the sobs slowed to ragged hiccups. Kelsey pulled slowly away from me, brushed the blonde hair out of his face, and rubbed his red eyes.

"Where have you been hiding?" I asked him.

His voice broke again and I thought he wasn't going to be able to answer, but he pulled himself together. "Under cottages."

A pair of sea gulls flew overhead, landing on top of a large dumpster next to a run-down guesthouse across the street. "You can't be doing that, Kelsey. How old are you anyway?"

"Thirteen."

Thirteen. Christ, he was young. Too young to be on the beach alone, especially with night coming. "Look, you can't be hiding under cottages. It'll be dark soon. The police just want to help you. Why don't you let me walk you down the police station?" The station was only a short distance away on Ashworth Avenue.

"No! They'll put me in a foster home." The boy looked terrified and I didn't really blame him.

"What about your father? Relatives? You got anyone I could call for you?"

Kelsey shook his head.

"The police are going to catch up with you sooner or later. The beach isn't very big, you know that. Come on, I'll walk you down there. They'll ask you some questions about your mom's...ahhh...accident and then they'll find you a nice family to stay with." I wasn't sure about that last part, but what else can you say to a thirteen-year-old kid? I couldn't leave him on the street, especially with night coming. Hampton's safe as far as beaches go but it's not that safe. And things are worse in the off-season. Wherever the cops placed him couldn't be any worse than where he was now.

Kelsey straightened up. He gripped his skateboard so tightly I thought he was going to snap it in two. "It wasn't an accident. My mom wouldn't do that. She wouldn't leave me alone like this."

I felt bad for him. No thirteen-year old should be in the position he was in. "Kelsey, your mom was alone and some-times grownups make mistakes when they're alone."

"She wasn't alone. Someone was with her."

That surprised me. "Who?"

"I don't know."

"Was it a man or a woman?"

"I couldn't tell."

"What were they doing?"

Kelsey's face got red and he looked away from me. "Drinking, I guess. I stayed in my room. I could hear them. They were arguing. So I snuck out my window and went boarding. I do it a lot. When I came back later, I climbed back in through my window. I didn't hear anything so I went to sleep. When I woke up, that's when I saw Ma in the chair with her head on the table..."

He started to tear up, but forced himself to keep talk-ing. "I tried to wake her...I could tell she wasn't gonna wake up this time. And I remembered what Ma said about them taking me away to foster care. So I just skat-ed around the beach. I don't know how long. I knew she was...was...dead and I didn't know what to do. You were the only one who ever tried to help us, so finally I came to you."

The fact that Cora Sweeney hadn't been alone just before she died put a whole new light on the situation. Cora had said she'd had differences with people on the beach. Maybe there was a connection. "Did your mom have any problems with anyone lately?"

"Yes," Kelsey answered softly.

"With who?"

It took him a full minute to answer. "I don't wanna tell you. I'd probably get hit again."

"Kelsey, you trust me, don't you? I won't let anyone hurt you."

He gave me a long, frightened look, then finally said something so quietly I had to ask him to repeat it. "Lenny Quarters."

Lenny Quarters. I knew the name. He owned the big purple arcade on the south end of Ocean Boulevard. Of course, Quarters was just a nickname. His real last name was Conklin. "What problem did your mom have with Lenny Quarters? Because he hit you?"

The boy nodded. "Kinda. Someone kept breaking into his arcade and stealing from the machines."

I almost interrupted him to ask if he had done it, then realized it didn't make much difference.

"He thought Ma had me doing it. He told her to make me stop. It wasn't Ma. She'd never make me do something like that."

"The police'll want to know about Lenny Quarters."

The kid looked scared and shook his head. I couldn't tell who he was more scared of — Lenny Quarters or the cops.

"You're going to have to talk to them sooner or later," I said. "You can't live under cottages the rest of your life."

All of a sudden he looked at me like a man looks at a man and it startled me. "I know my mother. She'd never leave me alone. Something bad happened. The cops won't believe a kid. I want you to help me find out what happened to Ma."

Help him? The best way I could help him would be to turn him into the cops and get him off the streets. Folks call the beach Happy Hampton, but it's anything but happy when darkness falls during the off-season.

On the other hand, I wasn't sure he was wrong about someone else being there when his mother died. Although it probably was just another alcoholic buddy of hers who got scared and split when she died in front of him. Or maybe he left before she died.

A car screeched to a halt at the head of M Street up on Ocean. I looked around and saw a green-and-white Hampton police cruiser.

"Here," Kelsey said. He thrust something in my hand as a car door slammed. I looked back to see a cop standing beside the driver's door and when I turned back toward Kelsey, I was just in time to see him riding low on his board down the sidewalk, banging a left and disappearing down a driveway. No use following. By the time I got to the driveway, he'd be two streets away.

I headed back out to Ocean Boulevard. Looked like the cop hadn't noticed Kelsey after all. He was writing up a twenty-something who had a mean-looking pit bull on a long thick chain in one hand and an open container of Bud in the other hand. Odd that the pit bull was legal, but the Bud was not.

I resumed my interrupted walk home, staring at the four quarters Kelsey had shoved in my hand just as the cruiser had pulled up. Four quarters? Was this a down payment? After all, the boy had asked for my help.

I fingered the prescription bottle in my pants pocket. I was supposed to be avoiding stressful situations—doctor's orders—and this definitely fit the bill.

Then I remembered the promise I'd made to myself a while ago, a promise to never back out of anything because of fear alone. If I did, I'd never be able to tell the difference between a justified fear and an irrational fear conjured up by my anxiety condition. No way I wanted to spend my life needlessly running and hiding from everything that made me skittish. There had to be a real reason to turn away. I couldn't think of one. I'd brought this condition on myself, with too much coke, and I was going to beat it myself too. I pulled my hand away from one pocket and dropped the quarters into the other.

Chapter 6

THE PART OF THE BEACH I live on is referred to as the Island, a name it earned in the distant past because it is cut off from the rest of the beach's homes and businesses by Ocean Boulevard. The name hadn't been used in decades until recently, when it was resurrected by beach real estate agents and area property owners attempting to make the homes there more desirable to prospective buyers. The Island sits on the south end of the beach down near the state park and Hampton Bridge. The bridge stretches across the Hampton River and leads to Seabrook, New Hampshire, and Salisbury, Massachusetts, a short distance beyond. The Island consists of less than ten small streets, with maybe a couple hundred properties with cottages of differing sizes. Most of the streets begin up on Ocean Boulevard and end at the sand, running parallel to each other with River Street running through the middle of some of them. South of Boar's Head, the Island is the only section of Hampton with homes and cottages where you don't have to cross Ocean Boulevard to get to the beach. That's one of the reasons the area is prized in the summer as a rental spot for families with small children.

That's where I was now, sitting on the front porch of my cottage down on the Island. I'd bought the place back when I owned the High Tide and was doing pretty well. When my wife and I separated, she and the kids stayed with the house in Massachusetts and I got shuffled up here. I counted myself lucky though. If we hadn't had this cottage, I guess I could have wound up in a lonely hotel efficiency up on the strip or in some hovel down near Ashworth Avenue.

Anyway, my cottage is only a couple of cottages away from the sand. And even though you can't see the ocean, when the tide is high you can smell and hear the water like it's right outside your door. Being set back a bit from the water has an important advantage over the homes that sit right on the sand. Those homes can get hit pretty hard during the occasional bad Nor'easter the New Hampshire seacoast experiences. The cottages that stand between my property and the ocean have served as a protective barrier for decades.

It was nice just sitting in the dark on the porch, rocking back and forth, sipping on a cold Heineken, smelling the salty sea air, and listening to the sounds of the ocean rolling almost up to the dunes.

But no matter how nice it was sitting there and how relaxed I was beginning to feel sipping my third beer, I still couldn't get Kelsey Sweeney and the meeting I'd had with him a few hours ago out of my mind. I glanced down at the white plastic table beside me. Even in the dark I could see the four quarters the boy had thrust into my hand.

I felt bad for him. How could anyone not? But his situation didn't have much to do with me. After all, I'd just met the boy. If I got involved with the personal problems of half the down-on-their-luck people on the beach, I'd be up to my neck in grief. Besides, hadn't Steve Moore told me that Cora Sweeney's death was a suicide or accidental overdose? He was the professional; he should know better than a scared kid who probably just wouldn't accept what had really happened.

I wasn't too concerned about the arguing Kelsey had heard. I could chalk that up to his mother and a boozy buddy of hers ranting and raving at each other. And when Cora passed out, whoever it was probably just panicked and took off. Sure, that was it. Things like that happened all the time at Happy Hampton Beach.

Still, I couldn't just leave the kid high and dry, sleeping under cottages every night. Maybe Steve Moore could steer me in the direction of whatever state agency took care of kids like Kelsey. Kids who have no one left to care about them. I just wanted to make sure he got taken care of right and didn't get dumped in some hellhole.

That's all I needed to do — help Kelsey get off the streets and into somewhere half-decent. Only there was something else I had to consider: that damn vow I'd made to myself. I'd been staying away from the cocaine, although it was a daily struggle. Harder was dealing with the fear the panic attacks generated. I'd had to force myself to face situations that brought on anxiety and sometimes the attacks. And if I hadn't done that, I'd have probably ended up like a hermit crab, hunkered down in my little cottage. So I'd placed myself in a lot of uncomfortable positions, ones that would have seemed like nothing to a normal person, even though sometimes I'd needed the pills or beer to get through them. I hadn't ever knowingly backed away from anything just because of my anxiety condition. And I wasn't going to now. I wasn't going to end up an agoraphobic, peeking out of my cottage window like I was jacked up on blow again.

The only problem with this line of thinking was that sometimes I couldn't tell if I was steering clear of something because it was the normal thing to do or because my anxiety was putting just enough of an edge on my system to keep me away from it. Telling which was which turned out to be the toughest part of all. So I'd made myself the promise: if I was ever in doubt about how I was acting toward a situation, even if I had a small suspicion that I was gun-shy because of the abnormal anxiety, then I had to face the situation and follow wherever it led. That was the only way I figured I could ever hope to beat this condition.

And so that's why I was stuck with this Kelsey Swee-ney thing. I was pretty sure Cora Sweeney's death was either suicide or accidental overdose, as Steve Moore had suggested. But I wasn't that sure. I added the arguing Kelsey heard to what Cora Sweeney herself had told me about having difficulties with someone, and I ended up with a tickle of doubt in my mind. How could I walk away from the puzzle now? I'd never be sure why I walked away. Besides, Kelsey needed my help.

And somewhere deep down I realized another truth: I needed Kelsey's help too. I had a son and daughter, both about Kelsey's age. I rarely got to see them. That wasn't their fault. It wasn't my ex-wife's fault. It was my fault. I had no doubt about that. I had a lot of wrongs to right before I would have a chance to get them back in my life. I wasn't sure if I ever would. But I'd been trying my best for a while now and I was not going to give up. And sometimes when I looked at Kelsey I saw my own children standing there. When that happened, somehow I knew helping Kelsey would help me right one of those wrongs. I had to grab every one of those chances I could.

I sat there on the porch of my cottage—looking at the full moon, smelling the salt air, listening to the thunder of the surf, killing my third Heineken—and made a decision. Tomorrow I'd do something to help the boy. What, I didn't know. But a lot of times if you sleep on a question, you have the answer in the morning. So that's what I did. I slept on it.

Chapter 7

THE ANSWER I HAD the next morning was one I hadn't expected—Lenny Quarters. On the other hand, maybe I shouldn't have been surprised. After all, his was the only name that'd come up in this matter so far. Lenny "Quarters" Conklin. I didn't know the man personally, but I knew who he was—the owner of the Lenny Land arcade, a garish purple building on the south end of Ocean Boulevard. A joint that was stuffed to bursting with quarter and half-buck pinball and video games. I'd heard it was very lucrative.

I knew if I went poking around up there, I'd probably just be asking for trouble. But I had no choice. I was determined to check into this thing, both for Kelsey's sake and mine.

That's how I found myself standing on the sidewalk staring up at a two-story purple building with the words *Lenny Land* splashed across its face. A series of large overhead doors opened the front of the building like a mechanic's garage, only I heard the sounds of bells and whistles from the machines inside instead of engines and air compressors. I took a deep breath and went in.

The place was fairly crowded and plenty noisy considering it was morning and still off-season. The arcade had everything a thousand other arcades had—lots of teenagers, video and pinball machines, a change booth, and floor walkers. I buttonholed one of the walkers. He was a tall geek about twenty with bad skin. He had on a purple shirt with *Lenny Land* emblazoned on the pocket.

"I want to talk to Lenny."

He gave me a who-the-hell-are-you look, pretty much like I'd expected.

"I own the High Tide Restaurant," I lied. On the beach owning anything separates you from 99 percent of the people and gives you a bit of status. The geek nodded and I followed him to the rear of the arcade and a door marked "Office." The geek left and I knocked on the door.

"Come in."

I entered, closing the door behind me.

The office was a good-size one but there wasn't much to it. There was a file cabinet with a portable TV on top, a new but cheap-looking sofa, a couple of fold-out chairs, and a large metal desk with a man sitting behind it looking at me. He was bald with a ring of dark hair around the sides of his head. He had on a purple *Lenny Land* shirt too, probably size double extra large.

He motioned for me to sit, but otherwise he didn't seem overly friendly. "Something I can do for you?"

"My name's Dan Marlowe. I'm up at the High Tide," I said, trying to keep my position vague.

"Yeah, I thought you looked familiar. You used to own the place before you got screwed up, didn't ya? Now whattaya doing? Washing dishes or something, aren't ya?"

Needless to say, I didn't like this guy right off the bat. "I'm a bartender."

Lenny shook his round head. "Must be tough. Losin' a business like that. Christ, that'd be like me working out on the floor here and one a those kids out there, sitting in here, being my boss. I'd shoot myself first."

"Don't let me stop you."

Neither of us spoke for a minute. The metal chair was getting uncomfortable, so I started over again. "I just want to ask you a couple of questions if you don't mind?"

Lenny folded his hands and put them on top of his bald head. "Go ahead, shoot. But hurry up. I gotta count my money."

I didn't know whether he was joking or not. "It's about Cora Sweeney. Down off Ashworth. The woman they found dead?"

He nodded vigorously. "Yeah, yeah, yeah. I heard about her. Lady in the wheelchair. Boozer. Killed herself, didn't she?"

"Well, maybe. Police think so anyway. Did you know her?"

He still had his hands folded on his head and wasn't showing any emotion. At least not that I could pick up on. "How the hell would I know her?"

I was inexperienced at this, but I had an inside lead. "Her son says you knew her."

Lenny's expression changed just a bit. He stared at me and for an instant I thought he might come around the table after me. Finally he said, "What about it?"

"He also says you slapped him around." I kept an eye on Lenny's face. He didn't look upset. Not yet. If anything, he looked...self-righteous.

"So what? The punk deserved it."

"Why?" This Lenny Quarters was an asshole, that was for sure. But a big enough asshole to murder a lady in a wheelchair? I couldn't tell yet.

"I'm running a business here. I can't let kids get away with breaking into my machines every night like I'm holding their personal piggy banks. If the cops can't take care of it, I got to."

I felt my anger rising. "So you threatened Cora Sweeney? Told her she better get her kid to knock it off?"

His face collapsed. He took his hands off his head and placed them, palms down, on the desk. "Look. You make it sound worse than it was. Sure, I told her to control her kid. Who wouldn't in my situation?"

"And the breaks continued?"

"Goddamn right they continued."

"How do you know it was her kid?"

"If it wasn't him, he knows who it was. Those winter kids all run together."

"Did you tell the police about this disagreement you had with Cora Sweeney?"

He flipped his palms up. "Why should I? It was nothin'. Why would I want to get myself involved?"

"Maybe you wouldn't if you had something to hide." My voice cracked and my palms were sweating. I wasn't used to accusing someone of murder.

He craned his big squash across the table towards me. "Something to hide? What the fuck are you talkin' about? You think the broad was murdered or something? You think I did it?"

I shrugged and brushed the pill bottle in the pocket of my jeans.

Conklin's brow furrowed deeply. "Look. I don't want to open a can of worms with the cops. Sure, I wanted the breaks here to stop. But we're only talking about a fistful of quarters. I do pretty good here." He waved his hand around. "Do you think I need to kill someone over a few crummy quarters?"

I had to admit he probably didn't. Sure people had killed before over peanuts, but usually people who were desperate for dough. And I didn't think Lenny Quarters was all that desperate. There wasn't an arcade on the beach that wasn't a money-maker and he owned one of the biggest. Still, people do strange things when their business is threatened. "It must've cost you more than a few quarters to get the broken machines fixed."

"Yeah, it did. But not enough to do what you're implying. Besides, insurance covered some."

"Where were you late Tuesday night, early Wednesday morning?" Now I really sounded like a bad TV cop.

I could tell that his mind was spinning like one of the pinball machines out front. "I was here until closing at midnight like I am every night. Then I went home. Now if you're done playing detective, I got work to do."

I must have been done. I couldn't think of anything else to ask him. "I guess that's it."

"Why are you so interested in this broad anyway, Marlowe?"

"I'm a friend of the family." I guess that was true enough.

"How about keeping my name out of it. I got enough problems running this place without having some dead drunk cripple causing me trouble."

"Yeah, sure, Lenny," I said, standing up and looking down at him. "There's just one more thing. If you ever bump into the kid again, keep your hands off him."

He grunted.

I walked out of the office, back through the arcade with all the bells and whistles, and out onto Ocean Boulevard.

Outside the sun was shining and there were a lot of fair weather clouds. I stood for a minute looking at them, trying to figure out what, if anything, I'd learned from my talk with Lenny Quarters. Not much. He had a reason to get hot with Cora Sweeney, that was for sure. But like he'd said, it wasn't much of a reason. And surely not a big enough reason to force or encourage a person to take a bottle of pills and wash them down with booze.

If someone had helped Cora Sweeney exit this life, that's how they'd done it. I knew that now. Whether they had just encouraged a drunken Cora to take a few more pills than she needed or shoved them forcibly down her throat. Either way, it was homicide.

Chapter 8

I HAD TO TALK to someone about what I was getting myself involved in and maybe get a little help, too. There was one obvious choice—Shamrock Kelly. Shamrock and I were tight and we went way back. Even had some fun times before my life went sour. The man had stood by me during that time when many others hadn't. He could be trusted. And if anyone farted the wrong way on Hampton Beach, he knew about it. He also had a tiny place out on one of the back streets near Cora Sweeney's and was familiar with a lot of the winter people who lived down there.

So after my talk with Lenny Quarters, I popped into the Tide and mentioned to Shamrock that I'd like to talk to him. We agreed to meet that night at his favorite watering hole, The Crooked Shillelagh, which was a few blocks from the High Tide.

Shamrock showed up at the Shillelagh a few minutes past the hour and joined me at a little table up near the bar. If I hadn't known better, I might have thought a large version of an Irish leprechaun was sitting across from me. The leprechaun ordered Guinness; I was drinking Black & Tans.

Trying to have a conversation above the music from a four-piece Irish band was like trying to wash laundry in a mud hole. A young woman was fronting the band, singing and playing a mean fiddle. Freckles and bright red hair set off a good-looking face with a body to match. I glanced around, peering through the smoke at all the Irish signs, photos, and ephemera hanging from the walls. Every voice I heard in the place, employees and customers, had a brogue to one degree or another.

Finally the band took a break and I got down to business with Shamrock. "Did you know the lady who died the other day out back?"

Shamrock brought the pint he was working on down from his lips, leaving a beer mustache across his upper lip. "Is the pope Catholic? 'Course I knew her. I know everybody."

"How well did you know her?"

He shook his head. "Not well, Danny boy. Not really. The poor soul didn't get about much. She was in a wheelchair."

"Yeah, I know. Her boy asked me to help him find out about his mother's death. He's a young kid, Shamrock. About the same age as my boy."

Shamrock looked genuinely sad, like only the Irish can do. "That was the lad that came to the bar the other morning, Danny? I saw him. I knew something was wrong. Poor boy. But what can you do? His dear mother took her own life, did she not?"

"Her boy doesn't think so. He heard her arguing with someone the night she died. And she'd told me she was having trouble with at least one person on the beach."

Shamrock looked puzzled. "You knew her from before?"

I didn't want to get into the High Tide break. "Yeah, but not good."

He didn't look satisfied, but he didn't push it. "You think someone done her in?" he whispered.

I nodded. "Maybe, Shamrock, maybe. I told the boy I'd look into it."

Shamrock lifted the pint to his mouth and drained the glass. He signaled for another round. "So what can I do to help?"

"You know a lot of people down there. I was thinking maybe you can pick up on any scuttlebutt that might be going around about Cora Sweeney or her son Kelsey."

"Of course I can. I'll be glad to do it. Especially for a young lad with an Irish name like Sweeney. If anyone blew their nose twice near him or his mother, Michael Kelly will find out about it." He patted his chest.

If anyone could get the info I needed, Shamrock could. But I didn't want him getting carried away. The police wouldn't appreciate him poking his nose into what they probably considered police business and I wasn't sure what we were really dealing with here. "You've got to be discreet, Shamrock. I don't want anyone else getting hurt or in trouble with the cops."

He held his hand up and made it shimmy. "Don't you worry. I'm Mr. Discreet. But if there was any funny business going on, I'll find out."

I felt a twinge of guilt at the thought that I might be pointing Shamrock in the direction of trouble. After all, I'd known he wouldn't refuse me a favor. I probably would have paid more attention to that little twinge, but the barmaid came with our beers and the band took the stage again.

Chapter 9

THE NEXT MORNING when I got up and stepped out on the porch, the beach was socked in with fog. You couldn't see much but the fog kept the temperature nice and cool—good running weather. So I shook off a hangover, put on running shoes and shorts, and went for a jog on the hard sand, something I tried to do every other morning.

When I got back to the cottage, I took a shower and dressed quickly. I had somewhere I wanted to visit before work—Cora Sweeney's street. I had no idea what I'd be looking for or what I was planning to do once I got there. For some reason I felt I had to get another look at the area. So I made the short walk across Ocean Boulevard, down a lettered street, and along Ashworth.

Cora's dead-end street looked the same as the last time I'd been there. The same run-down cottages, each with overflowing rubbish barrels out front. Fortunately, I didn't see any mutts around this time, but I kept a wary eye out for them. I studied Cora Sweeney's home as I strolled past, and if I hadn't already known about the recent death there, I'd never have learned it by looking at the place. Nothing seemed unusual. I don't know what I expected to see—maybe leftover yellow police tape or something. On second thought, there would be no tape if the police felt there was no foul play involved.

Suddenly, I felt foolish. What did I know? I had no experience with this sort of thing.

I turned around at the end of the short street and was on my way back, almost abreast of the Sweeney place, when a faint click-clicking caught my attention. On the other side of the street, up on a porch, sat an old woman in a rocking chair. If she'd been there on my first pass, I hadn't noticed her. She had white hair piled on her head, bun-style. She was knitting up a storm and it was the needles I'd heard. I walked over toward the woman and put one foot up on her porch step. I hate to use this description but all I can say is she looked like something out of the Appalachian Mountains.

"Good morning," I said. She didn't answer right away, just looked up at me. The knitting needles were flying so fast in her fingers I was surprised they weren't emitting sparks.

Finally, she spoke. She even sounded like she was from the mountains. "You been a lookin' at Cora's place."

I hadn't thought I'd been that obvious. "Well, yeah. I guess I have."

"You know'd her?" She turned her head a bit as if she was studying me with just one eye. Maybe her better one?

"Yes, I did." Well, that wasn't a lie. I had met her, after all.

"Come on up here. Talk a bit." She patted the seat of a rocker beside her. I took her up on the invitation. The rocking chair was comfortable, one of those old wooden ones that every porch on the beach used to have years ago. Now I'd be lucky to find one at an antique store, and they'd want an arm and a leg for it.

"My name's Mattie Morrison. Short for Matilda. What's yours, son?"

"Dan. Dan Marlowe."

"Dan. That's a strong name. So you were a friend of Cora's." She kept knitting as she talked, but I didn't find it distracting now. Strangely, the action seemed somehow soothing, the soft click of the needles and the smoothness and speed with which her hands moved. My ex-wife knitted and just watching Mattie knit reminded me of her.

"Well, not really a friend. I'd just met her recently. Her and her son."

The old woman nodded. "That'd be Kelsey. A good boy. But he had it hard living with his mother, her in that steel chair and...well, you probably know'd Cora liked her adult beverages. Still, she loved that boy more than anything and she tried to do the best she could for him under tryin' circumstances."

"Have you seen Kelsey lately?" I asked.

She shook her head. "Not since before he found his mother. You knew it was him who found her? Then he run away. Boy's probably plenty scared."

"Yes, I know that. He doesn't have anything to be afraid of though. The police just want to help him. Get him off the beach streets."

"It ain't just the police he's afraid of." Her knitting needles seemed to be moving faster now if that was possible.

"There's someone else he should be afraid of?" She didn't answer me, just kept those needles flying, and I figured I better not push that tack. So I tried another. "The police say she either took her own life or accidentally did too much liquor and pills."

Mattie Morrison suddenly dropped the needles on top of the yarn in her lap and grabbed both arms of her rocker, stopping it cold. "They're stupid or they lie. That woman would no more kill herself than I would. Especially with that boy. He meant everything to her. I know. I talked to Cora every day. She never woulda left him alone like this. Never."

"It could've been an accident though," I said.

"Not likely." She squeezed the arms of her rocker so tight her bony knuckles turned white. "Sure, she liked to drink. Everybody know'd that. But that made her a pro at it and pros don't make those mistakes, amatoors do."

I had to agree with that. All bartenders know that the most dangerous drinkers were the amateurs who came out occasionally, like on New Year's Eve, which was a good time for the more experienced drinker to stay home. "Could have been the pills though."

"No." She shook her head hard. "I told you we talked a lot and she told me about those pills a hers. Nerve pills, that's what they were. And lord knows a woman might need them down here alone in the winter. Especially with no man and in a chair like that. She told me she was very leery of them pills. Didn't like 'em, but hadda take 'em sometimes. Mostly in the winter, she said, when it gets awful dark and lonely out here. Even I gets a scared sometimes. She said she hardly ever took any of those pills when the good weather come."

"Like now?"

"Like now," Mattie nodded.

There was something else I'd forgotten to find out and I figured now was a good time to do it. "What about the boy's father?"

She harrumphed. "Ober Sweeney? If father's what you can call the man."

"What's the matter with him?"

"I don't wanna speak bad a no one, but him I will. After Cora's accident she got a nice little settlement. 'Course he stole it all. Spent it on that dope stuff, I heard. Got put in jail. Almost stayed in jail too. Judge let him out so he could make payments to Cora every month. Ha! He was supposed to pay for the boy too. Cora had trouble gettin' anything. She couldn't do much in that chair and all. Top it off, that peckerhead had lots a money sometimes."

"Lots of money? Where'd he get lots of money?" I asked.

"I dunno, but you can bet it wasn't on the up and up."

"Where's he live?"

"Seabrook, I think."

"Was she having problems with anyone else?"

"She said somethin' about her damn landlord. I dunno what. But she had a year-round lease and you know how those slumlords operate. Probably wanted to get the poor cripple outta there so he could rent to some fancy-pants tourist in the summer." She shook her snow-white head. "I don't have to worry about that, thank Jesus. I owned this place forever. Couldn't afford to buy it now."

I wanted to get back to what she'd said about Kelsey having more than the police to be afraid of so I tried to bring it up again but she shot me right down. "I gots to go in now, Dan. Got some things to do." She stood with her needles and yarn and I stood too. I was surprised to see how short she was. I'm six feet tall and beside her, I felt eight.

I had no idea what I might want to say to her in the future but I asked if she'd mind if I stopped by again to talk about Cora and Kelsey. She shook her head. "No, I don't mind. But you better hurry up. At my age, you never know." There wasn't a bit of fear in her voice and she let out a sweet little chuckle.

"All right, Mrs. Morrison. Thanks for the talk. It was nice to meet you."

She reached out, touched my hand, and said, "Mattie, Dan, Mattie." Then she wished me good luck, for what I didn't know, and went inside.

I clomped down the steps and headed up the street toward Ashworth, thinking about what Mattie had said about Ober Sweeney stealing his crippled wife's settlement, then stiffing her on paying that same settlement back. The child support too. What kinds of things would a dirtbag like that do to get out of forking over all that money? Maybe murder?

I'd just reached Ocean Boulevard when I remembered what Mattie Morrison had said about landlords wanting winter people out when the good weather came so they could get the high-paying vacationers' money. I knew most of the winter people did have to leave for the summer, for just that reason. What about Cora Sweeney and Kelsey? Had their landlord wanted them out even though they had a year-round lease? How did someone go about checking up on something like that? I scowled and made a mental note to look into the Sweeney's lease situation later as I turned the corner and headed towards the High Tide.

Chapter 10

I WAS LATE when I reached the High Tide. Dianne was doing prep work on the speed table when I walked into the kitchen. Guillermo, the head chef, was on the other side fooling around with the fryolators. Dianne glanced up; she didn't say anything.

"Sorry. I had to help a friend with a problem," I half-lied. She nodded. I was hardly ever late, so everyone assumed if I was, I had a good reason. I often joked with the staff that my motto was 'Come in early, leave on time.' I followed that motto pretty religiously, too.

There was no sign of Shamrock in the bar area when I went out, although I could tell he'd been there. I noticed an empty donut box and a newspaper clipping of the day's lottery numbers on top of a rack of clean bar glasses. On the other side of the wooden partition I could hear a couple of the waitresses chattering away as they did their table and station setups. Usually, I'd at least peek my head around the partition and say hi. This morning I didn't. I had too much on my mind. And it wasn't all about Cora and Kelsey Sweeney, Mattie Morrison, Steve Moore, Lenny Quarters, Ober Sweeney, and Shamrock either. It was more about my family — what I had left of it.

My ex-wife, Sharon, and I had finally bitten the bullet and gone through with the divorce. Or more accurately, I'd bitten the bullet. She'd been pushing for that divorce for a long time and I couldn't blame her. I'd just held out hope that the more time that passed, the better the chance she'd see that I'd gotten my demons under control and my life back on track. She hadn't ended up convinced of either. Neither had I for that matter.

We'd settled everything financially. She kept the house in Massachusetts, I got the small beach cottage. Both were heavily mortgaged. Still, we were lucky we hadn't lost them. I mean we were lucky *I* hadn't lost them. I'd lost almost everything else — my business, my family, my self-respect, and damn near my life. My health was a little shaky, too. And it was tough getting enough money together to send her the monthly check and still have enough to keep my creditors happy up here. But so far so good. If worse came to worse, I could sell the cottage and move into a small place out back like Shamrock. Hell, I'd lived in a place like that before I'd been married, and I could do it again if I had to.

The one thing I swore I would never do is fail to get that money to Sharon. No way were my kids ever going to have to leave their home because of me. I didn't care if I had to eat sand. After all, the break-up had been my fault. The whole freakin' thing had been my fault.

I still held out some hope that if I could just hang in there, I could get my family back. It wouldn't be soon. But if I could just hold myself together long enough, I could build my life back up again. Maybe somehow scrape together enough to buy back the Tide or another place like it. If Sharon saw that I had worked hard enough to get the restaurant back and that I was on track and that I meant to stay that way, she might be willing to try again. No matter what she said I knew she still had some feelings for me.

That's why I got up every day — to win back my wife and kids. And to do that I had to regain my dignity. But every day was a struggle. I knew that time was supposed to make everything better, but I hadn't reached that point yet. Someday I hoped I would. I had to think that way. Otherwise, they'd find me in my cottage just like Cora Sweeney. With only one difference — there'd be no doubt what had happened to me.

A shout from the kitchen caught my attention before I could go down that dark road.

"Dan, can you come in here? Dan?" It was Dianne's voice.

I pushed through the swinging doors into the kitchen. Dianne and Guillermo were still where I'd last seen them—Diane at the speed table close to the doors and Guillermo over by the fryolators. Only this time they both had their hands over their heads and were staring at a figure at the other end of the kitchen—a man with a stocking mask over his face and a long-barreled pistol in his hand. He waved the pistol at me. I put my hands in the air, imitating Diane and Guillermo.

"You two over there." His hard, gravelly voice fit his body nicely. He wore a lightweight jacket zipped to his chin. Dianne and I followed his instructions and moved behind the speed table. He motioned with the gun for Guillermo to back up toward us.

The beach isn't known for armed robberies; they're rare. Lots of break-ins, but hardly ever a stickup, at least not until today.

"Where's everyone else?" The masked man walked around the other end of the speed table and stood between it and the fryolators, gun still pointed at us.

"It's just us," Dianne answered, her voice cracking. I struggled not to stare at her and listened for the waitresses out front. They must've run out of things to say—I couldn't hear a thing.

"Good. This'll be easy."

"You picked the wrong time of day to rob us," I said. "But the little that's here is out in the registers."

The gunman snickered. "Not only have ya got a big nose, Marlowe. You're a stupid bastard, too. I ain't here for no dough. I'm here to give ya a message."

A message? "I don't know what you're talking about."

"You been bothering people on the beach with your questions. Stirring up trouble where there weren't none before. I want it stopped."

Now I got it. I turned my head slightly. Dianne's and Guillermo's hands were still over their heads. I could actually see Dianne's fingers shaking. Guillermo hadn't said a word yet and I didn't think it was because of his mediocre English. His eyes looked like black olives, and suddenly I thought about how ironic it would be if he died here in a Hampton Beach kitchen when years before he'd barely torn off his army uniform in time to get out of Managua before the Sandinistas marched in.

"Hey, Marlowe." The gunman waved his pistol. "Ya hear me or ya got wax in your ears?"

I wasn't going to play hero. I had a gun pointed at me and besides Dianne and Guillermo were my friends; I didn't want them harmed. Yeah, I was scared too. Time to tell this character what he wanted to hear. "I heard you. I won't be bothering anybody. You got my word on that."

"Word? You're makin' this seem too easy, Marlowe. You're a pussy and a junkie but even you wouldn't roll over this fast. And besides, I wanna earn my money." He took two steps toward us.

The name calling didn't hurt. I'd been called worse. Beside me Dianne let out a soft whimper—that did hurt. Out of the corner of my eye I saw the row of metal pots--my weapon of choice when I'd been checking out the break--hanging within reach. How long would it take to grab one of those pots and coldcock the guy? Probably long enough for him to get a couple of slugs in me and have a cup of coffee to boot.

"You win," I said, and I meant it. "You're not going to have any more trouble with me. It's none of my business anyhow."

"For some reason I don't believe you, Marlowe. I think you need to know we're serious."

He covered the last few steps with lightning speed, lowering his gun as he came. When he got within reach, the gun flashed upward, connecting with flesh and bone with a sickening thud. For an instant I thought he'd hit Dianne. She grabbed her face and screamed, staring at Guillermo who staggered backward and dropped to the floor. The gun'd smashed into his lower jaw. I could tell by the sound they'd have to wire it up.

I moved toward the gunman, but he swung the gun around quickly, put the pistol to my chest, and gave me a shove back. I glanced down at Guillermo. He was holding his jaw with both hands, blood running between his fingers. At the same time he was giving up his breakfast.

The gunman waved his pistol again. Diane put her hands back above her head. I raised my hands higher. "Now Marlowe. I don't even know this wetback. See what I done to him? Imagine what I'd do to you."

I tried my best to convince him I was through playing detective. "All right. All right. You convinced me. I won't be a problem." I didn't sound believable even to me.

"Marlowe, Marlowe. You just don't sound like you mean it." His eyes flicked toward Dianne. I knew instantly what that meant. And I couldn't let it happen.

Just as his gun hand started to move, the kitchen doors banged open and two female voices started shouting. The waitresses had heard Dianne's scream.

The gunman shot a glance at the door, turned his gun in that direction. I saw my chance and grabbed his gun wrist with both of my hands, forcing both the gun and his hand high over our heads. I pushed hard and he stumbled backwards toward the fryolators. Someone screamed behind me. Our faces were so close I could smell his breath, rancid as bad meat, through the stocking mask.

He clubbed me in the side with his left fist, trying to get me to release my hold. I clung to his gun hand in spite of the pain. Letting go wasn't an option. He twisted his wrist in my hand, trying to turn the gun so he could get a shot at my head. I ducked and shoved his gun hand higher. He aimed some knuckle blows to my ribs with his free hand, blows that left me gasping for breath. My vision had started to darken and I could feel my hands slipping when the blows suddenly stopped. I glanced over. Dianne stood on the other side of the gunman, clinging to his free arm for dear life. He tried to shake her free, but she must've yanked hard at the same instant I did and he stumbled to his knees.

I stood over him, still holding his gun wrist with both hands. Just inches below that gun hand sat a fryolator with its greasy contents at a rolling boil. This time I was in control. He knew it too. His eyes were as big as sand dollars.

I didn't stop to think. The gun barrel went in first. He struggled and I pushed harder. I could still hear Guillermo moaning and thought of what the gunman had tried to do to Dianne.

"Stop, Marlowe. Don't do it." His voice didn't sound so hard anymore.

"Screw you," was all I said.

One of the boiling grease bubbles popped and hit his knuckles. The gunman let out a cry and dropped the gun. It disappeared into the grease. Dianne clung to his other arm like a rag doll as he tried to throw her off. I brought all my weight down on his hand, shoving it into the boiling grease all the way up to within an inch or two of my hands. The grease sizzled and the stench of frying flesh rose to my nose.

The man twisted and bucked like a horse that had been stung by a bee, managing to throw me back into the speed table, breaking my hold on his wrist. Dianne sat on the floor, staring as the gunman raced toward the back door.

I dashed after him, but by the time I was through the door and outside, he was already jumping into an older model car parked a few yards away on the adjacent side street. The car peeled out. I ran after it but couldn't get the plate number.

Back inside the place was in an uproar. Dianne was still sitting on the kitchen floor, but now she held Guillermo's head in her lap. She stroked his curly black hair, talking softly to him. They were both covered in blood. Guillermo's blood. He was conscious, and even with all the blood I could tell that — except for the wiring job and a nice scar — eventually he'd be ok.

One waitress was hysterical. The other was probably out in the dining room calling the cops.

A few minutes later, I heard the wail of sirens. Usually no one pays attention to sirens here on the beach. They're like the boy who cried wolf — hear them too many times and everyone stops paying attention.

This time I paid attention, though. This time I knew where they were going.

Chapter 11

NATURALLY I DIDN'T SLEEP too good that night. Beer didn't help; neither did a Xanax. The realization that Kelsey Sweeney was probably right about his mother's death put me in a bind. When Shamrock came back to the Tide, I'd pulled him aside and told him about the muscle with the gun. This thing had escalated beyond just asking a few questions and now Shamrock and I were both in danger. The smart side of my brain knew I should stay out of whatever was going on. But the not-so-smart side realized that Kelsey Sweeney was in even worse danger.

All night I couldn't shake the nagging vision of what would happen when whoever was behind all this violence caught up to Kelsey. Maybe that's why I chose to ignore the gunman's warning—my concern for the boy. Or maybe I was just stupid. Or maybe it was the beer and pills. Anyway, the next morning I popped another pill for medicinal reasons and faced the day.

Mattie Morrison had pointed me in a direction I could take action on. It wasn't hard to find where Ober Sweeney lived. I just looked the name up in the phone book and there was his address. The guy lived in Seabrook all right. Today was Sunday, one of my days off this week, so I decided to drive over the Hampton Bridge in that direction.

I had a nice view of the Atlantic Ocean on my left and the domed Seabrook Nuclear Power Plant on my right as I cruised across the bridge. The plant was beyond the harbor and marsh; the sun glinting off the plant's surface made the facility look strangely attractive, just like it did at night when the monstrosity was all lit up like a Christmas tree. I hated the place. But like most people on the beach I'd learned to live with it.

I got over the bridge and kept on Route 1A until I took a right onto 286. It wasn't long before I came to the street I was looking for. Ober Sweeney's road was all dirt with enough ruts and rocks to make an off-roader happy. I'd only gone a short distance before I was leaving a dust cloud behind me.

About a hundred yards in I came to a trailer on a foundation. The place was a run-down mess with debris scattered all over the yard. A stripped car, probably standard issue in this neighborhood, sat beside the trailer.

I couldn't even make out what kind it was. A pickup, which I assumed ran but didn't look much better than the car, was parked in front of the trailer. I pulled my car up beside the pickup and got out. I glanced around, half-expecting to be attacked by vicious dogs, but none materialized.

Three wooden steps led to the trailer's door. I stood on the first step and knocked. What the hell was I going to say to this man when he answered? I hadn't come just to ask about his ex-wife, but about Kelsey, too. His son. Did Ober Sweeney know the boy was running around the beach without a place to sleep? He had to know. The police must have told him. Or maybe they hadn't. Or maybe he didn't care.

"Whatcha want?"

I spun around. I didn't know where the guy behind me had come from but he stood barely ten feet away, staring at me as if I was a child molester come to rent a room. He looked like a hundred other guys I'd seen through the years. His tattoos and long red ponytail told me he'd probably been a big tough biker at one time. Now all I saw standing in front of me was a jerky skeleton. I didn't have to be a Narc to realize what kind of dope Mattie Morrison had been talking about.

I came down off the step. "Ober Sweeney?"

"What the fuck do you want?"

That threw me. Even though the guy was skinny, and I could probably handle him if I had to, I wasn't sure he didn't have a weapon. A familiar feeling started to build inside me. I ignored my suddenly sweaty palms and cleared my throat. "I'd like to talk to you for just a minute."

"Get the fuck outta here. You ain't a cop and I don't talk to bill collectors."

I stared as the man's face started to move in a series of facial tics too numerous to count. "I'm here about your son, Kelsey."

For a moment even the tics stopped and it looked like Sweeney was either thinking hard or trying to. What ran through the brain of a man like that when he was thinking hard was a conundrum to me.

"What about him?" Sweeney finally said.

"Did you know his mother died?"

He got defensive. "Of course I did. The pigs were here. They told me she killed herself. Stupid bitch. Ends up in a wheelchair and then offs herself. I told her she would do something like that sooner or later."

"Did you know your son's living outside on the beach somewhere?"

"Yeah, they told me that too. So what? What the hell's that to me? The kid never listened to me anyhow. Besides, he can take care of hisself. I showed him how." He straightened his scrawny shoulders.

"He's only thirteen."

Sweeney smirked. "So what?"

I looked at his lined face and shaking hands. The kid was probably better off sleeping in the sand under a cottage than with this dirtbag. So why the hell was I trying to talk to him about the boy? "Did you see your ex-wife much?"

"Anything was too much."

"Had you seen her lately?"

His facial tics started to dance again. "What are ya doing, a sex survey or something? You a damn pervert? You ain't a damn cop, so get the hell outta here."

I wasn't planning on ever coming back and talking to this loser again if I could help it, so I ignored him and pushed on. "So you did see her."

He leered and said, "Hey, the bitch called me. Not the other way round. Sure, she was in a wheelchair but she still needed a man once in a while." He straightened his shoulders again. "She couldn't be choosy and she could still do things, ya know. And besides, she always had some free booze around."

"She have any enemies?"

"She was too stupid to have enemies."

Seemed like I was getting nowhere fast. Might as well ask this asshole about something else Mattie Morrison had pointed out. "I heard she lived at that cottage year round. This year too?"

His tics started to jitterbug. "How the hell would I know?"

I didn't believe him. There was nothing more important to a winter person; she would've told him if the landlord was kicking her out. "Was the landlord bothering her or coming around?"

"If he was, it was probably just to tap her." He let out a dirty snicker.

"She have any steady boyfriends?"

"She was in a damn wheelchair, for Chrissake. Who the hell could she get? You maybe?" He grinned like the trench coat man at a peepshow.

"Were you over there the night she died?"

"Me? Whattaya sayin', you cocksucker? You sayin' I killed her? What the fuck would I wanna kill that douche-bag for? I wouldn't waste my time. And what the hell am I wastin' my time with you for anyway? Who the fuck are you anyhow? Get the fuck outta here." His tics had changed direction which probably meant the guy was capable of snapping at any time. No matter — I'd seen and heard all I could stomach.

I headed for my car with him right behind me. He was probably telling himself, in that cinder brain of his, that he was throwing me off his property. But that didn't bother me. What did bother me was that poor kid, Kelsey. A thirteen-year old boy homeless on the beach with a dead mother and a piece of shit for a father. The kid sure didn't have much to work with, did he?

Chapter 12

WHEN I GOT BACK TO HAMPTON I didn't go directly to my cottage. Something that Ober Sweeney had mentioned stuck in my mind and I wanted to follow up on it. I drove right past the beach and over to the town proper. I parked my car at the small Hampton town hall and went inside. It only took a few minutes of going through the property tax records to find out who owned Cora Sweeny's ramshackle place. It was listed as belonging to something called "Beautiful Beach Realty Trust." I smiled when I read that; someone had a sense of humor. But who was the slumlord? Neither of the cotton-headed clerks posted behind the counter could, or would, give me any help. That was okay. The name had to be public record somewhere and I was sure I could find the information.

After I left the town hall I took a leisurely ride up the coast through Rye, Portsmouth, and into Kittery, Maine. I didn't do anything except drive and think. When I finally got home a couple of hours later I was so relaxed it didn't even bother me to see what I knew was an unmarked Hampton police car in my driveway. I parked on the street so I wouldn't block it in.

When I reached my front porch, I found Steve Moore sitting in a rocking chair like he owned the place. Short-sleeved shirt, tie, and chinos—as usual. "Where you been, Dan?"

I sat in the rocker beside him. "For a drive. How long you been here?"

He smiled. "Not long. Where'd you drive to?"

"Up the coast. What's with the questions?"

He stopped smiling and brought the rocker to a halt. "Look, we got word you were out back on Reed Street nosing around, bothering people, and..."

I interrupted. "I wasn't bothering anyone. I talked to one person and she started the conversation."

"Well, someone saw you wandering around down there near Cora Sweeney's house talking to people and let us know. And just a bit ago we got a jingle from the assessor's office. They knew what happened at the Sweeney property, of course, and figured we'd want to know someone was asking about it. One of the old hens even took down your plate."

"Just like you said last time I saw you, a regular Peyton Place."

"Always has been, Dan. You should know that."

"Something to drink?" I asked. I was hoping he'd say yes; I felt the need for a beer coming on bad.

"No." His voice became more serious. "If it wasn't for what happened at the restaurant yesterday, we'd probably let it all slide. But the chief's got something against pistol-whipping on his beach. Might scare the tourists away, I guess. So he sent me to talk to you."

"Go ahead. I've got nothing to hide."

Steve cleared his throat, took out that notebook and pen again. "All right. I know it's all public record, but my question is: what are you doing rifling through the property files on the Sweeney cottage?"

I studied Steve's face. He looked more concerned than accusatory. Besides, the way things were going having some law enforcement on my side might come in handy. So I decided to tell him that Kelsey Sweeney had heard his mother arguing with someone the night she died.

Steve shrugged. "So what? She was a lush, Dan, and lushes are always arguing about something. They wouldn't think they were having fun if they weren't."

"Yeah, but this was on the night she died."

"Look, we got more fights and jams down in that area than waves on the ocean. Doesn't mean a thing. Besides, we got the report back—accidental overdose."

Why wasn't I surprised? Looked like I was losing the fight, but I had to give it another try. "Come on, Steve. The kid heard loud arguing and then she's dead a few hours later?"

"Who the hell do you think you are, Dan? Sherlock Holmes? So she was arguing with someone. Another juice head probably. And he either left before she croaked or got scared when she did and split." Steve tucked the notepad and pen back in his shirt pocket. "Either way, same diff. They come and go so fast on this beach, especially now with all the winters getting ready to leave. You'd never find out who was with her anyhow. And it doesn't matter now. Report says accidental overdose. The body's been released and they've probably already buried it. I guess she didn't want any services. So what we want from you is to stop playing Spenser and keep out of it."

We were sitting, rocking, like two old men. I looked at Steve. "So you don't make anything out of her telling me she was having trouble with someone or the kid hearing the arguing?"

"Just that she was having a problem with someone — like we all do — and arguing with someone else — like we all do. Especially when we drink."

"What about the black purse?"

"What about it?"

"Did you find it?"

He pulled out a pack of Winstons jammed tight behind the notebook, tapped one out, fired up. He took his time blowing smoke rings before he answered. "We found the purse. Still had a few bucks in it."

"Few bucks? Steve, I saw the roll. She took it out right in front of me. It was a lot more than a few bucks."

"You count it?"

I didn't bother to answer that.

"So she pulls out a roll. Christ, it was probably mostly ones for all you know. If someone ripped her off, they wouldn't have left anything behind. They would've taken it all, wouldn't they?"

He had a point, so I decided to try a different angle. "What about the jerk at the restaurant? He hurt Guillermo bad but he wasn't after him. The warning was for me. You know that."

Steve shook his head. "By now the whole beach knows it. You said he didn't mention anything about Cora Sweeney or her cottage. Right?"

My stomach clenched. I knew where he was headed. "Right," I answered reluctantly.

"So, there's no connection with the Sweeney thing. Sure, pistol-whipping's serious and we're going to get the bastard. But one thing's got nothing to do with the other."

I checked out Steve's face to see if he was serious. "You're kidding, right?"

He flashed me a look; he hadn't liked that.

And here I'd thought Steve was a reasonable guy — for a cop. "I start asking questions about what happened to Cora Sweeney, and before the words are out of my mouth, someone out of a '40s B movie starts waving a gun around in the High Tide and slugging chefs? What's wrong with that picture?"

Steve seemed pissed. "Probably plenty to you. But if you knew what really was going on around this beach, you'd have a different view."

That got my interest. "Like what?"

"Dope for one. More than even you know about." He gave me a look I didn't like. "Other things, too. Things I'm not supposed to talk about and I won't."

"So what's that got to do with whether Cora Sweeney was murdered or not?"

"Plenty. We figure that while you were asking your crazy Sweeney questions, you probably got too close to something shady going on or spooked someone with something to hide. But we don't believe your visitor had anything to do with the Sweeney thing. You just put your damn nose in where it didn't belong. And once whoever it was realizes it was just a stupid blunder by an amateur detective looking into nothing but the Sweeney woman's death, they'll forget about you." Steve wrapped up this little speech in a tone that told me the matter wasn't up for debate.

Seeing he didn't seem too hot over any of my ideas, I figured I had nothing to lose by asking him one more question. "You don't know who owns Cora Sweeney's cottage, do you?"

"No."

"Ever hear of Beautiful Beach Realty Trust?" I asked.

"Probably the same people that run Beautiful Beach Real Estate, the rental operation up near Boar's Head."

Steve did a quick double-take. "Now wait a second. I'm telling you — stay out of this and stop bothering people. It's a dead issue. No pun intended." He flipped his butt off the porch and got up to go. He was halfway down the stairs when he stopped and turned back. "If the kid told you about some argument, I guess that means you've seen him. How come you didn't grab him for us?"

"You ever try to catch a kid on a skateboard?"

Steve smiled and said, "We almost had him a couple of times, but you're right, he is fast on that damn thing." The smile faded. "But you know this beach isn't any place for a kid his age to be running around loose with no one taking care of him and nowhere to live. It's not like when we were kids. It was a different place then."

I nodded. He was right about that.

"So if the kid comes to you again, hold him for us. You won't be doing him a favor if you don't."

He was probably right about that, too.

Chapter 13

THE NEXT DAY WAS MONDAY and I had a treat this week—two days off in a row. Yeah, Steve Moore said to keep my nose out of the Cora Sweeney incident, but there were three reasons to stay in the game. Number one—I couldn't just leave Kelsey out there scared, living under cottages, believing someone had killed his mother. If I could find something to convince him it was just an accident, maybe he'd calm down, and we could get him off the streets into some type of decent situation. Number two—I wasn't buying Steve Moore's theory. Not yet anyway. Too many coincidences. Number three—if I didn't follow through on this thing, I'd never be sure if it wasn't the damn anxiety putting the brakes on. So I decided to make a late morning visit to Beautiful Beach Real Estate. I'd heard the name before; the place had been around a long time. But, for some reason, when I'd found out the owner of Cora's cottage was Beautiful Beach Realty Trust I hadn't put two and two together. Steve Moore had done that embarrassingly easy math for me.

It was a nice day so I decided to walk. The business was located about a mile up on the north end of the beach across from Boar's Head, a peninsula that jutted out from that area of the beach. The sun glistened on the water and the 70 degree temps had brought out a good amount of traffic for May. Cars stacked up bumper-to-bumper on Ocean Boulevard with the municipal and private parking lots filling up fast. The sidewalks were fairly crowded; not like a hot weekend in July or August when you'd have trouble getting through the crowd with a chain saw, but enough that you had to watch where you were going or risk bumping into a mom herding her kids. Most of the businesses were either open or getting ready to open on Memorial Day weekend, the unofficial start of summer.

The Casino marked the halfway point on my little excursion. The place is a local landmark. In the old days, the large two-story, two-block-long building hosted big bands, like Glenn Miller, in the Casino Ballroom on the top floor. In the sixties it was Janis Joplin and Jim Morrison. Today you can enjoy everything from comedians to country & western to rap artists. It's a small venue and oftentimes you can catch soon-to-be-famous performers on their way up the success ladder or already-famous ones on their way down.

The bottom floor of the Casino houses a couple dozen businesses, including fast-food shops, games of chance, beachwear and novelty joints, and even the Cow's Ass Leather Shop.

One thing that bugged me about the Casino was the shooting gallery they'd stuck out front and center some years ago. I've got nothing against shooting galleries. In fact, I'd given this particular one enough quarters through the years to open a coin-operated laundry. But the Casino — and the gallery — I passed almost every day during the summer. Hearing the inane chatter of the gallery's target mannequins day in and day out, I swear, by the end of every summer season, I could hear those blasted mannequins in my sleep.

However, today still being pre-season, even the piano player dummy hitting the keys every time some sharpshooter bull's-eyed him didn't bother me too much. When I came out the other end of the Casino, I stopped at the intersection at the corner of D Street and glanced back over my shoulder. The building could use a few gallons of paint and a facelift. Then it should be good for another 100 years. After all, what's Hampton Beach without the Casino?

I'm a pretty fast walker and it only took me about twenty minutes to reach Beautiful Beach Real Estate. The place was a converted cottage right on Ocean Boulevard facing the seawall across the street. It was a gray building with the business name in red script on a sign over the front door. The windows were plastered with sheets of paper offering cottages and apartments for sale or rent. I'd known the office would be open even though it was Monday. All real estate businesses on the beach are open weekends at least, starting March 1st, and then every day by May 1. And I hadn't been wrong. A large blue and white "OPEN" flag fluttered on a pole stuck on the front of the building. I went up to the door, opened it, and stepped in.

I was barely through the door before a female agent was on me like I was famous.

"Sir, come right this way. Please take a seat." She was dressed in a sailor-type outfit—white top with little anchors on it and navy blue slacks—and looked like somebody's grandmother. Judging by the looks of her iron gray hair she more than likely got a perm once a week just like my mother had done. She attempted to steer me to a chair in front of the desk she'd sprung up from when I'd entered.

I pricked her balloon right away. "I already own a place on the beach and I'm not selling or renting." Her face collapsed like a dynamited building. "What I'd like to do is talk to the owner."

The woman's whole demeanor changed. "Well, I see. That'd be Mr. Norris. He's probably busy, but I suppose I can check."

I stood in the middle of the office while she knocked on a door, went in and closed the door behind her. I passed the time perusing the chintzy-looking diplomas and photos of two-bit politicians adorning the walls.

Who was still influenced by that kind of junk? I wondered. Then decided I didn't want to know. In a few minutes she came out.

"Mr. Norris will see you now," she said in a tone suggesting I was being granted an audience with the king.

I walked into the owner's office. Overflowing file cabinets leaned against walls papered with twins of the diplomas I'd seen out front with the addition of real estate plaques and awards. Standing behind a metal desk strewn with papers was a man of medium height. He had a shock of pure white hair, big-rimmed glasses, a gaudy sports coat, paisley tie, and a patent leather belt that matched his hair. I wouldn't have trusted this guy from here to the ocean.

He reached across the desk, grabbed my hand and jerked it up and down like a well pump. "Ted Norris, Ted Norris. Glad to meet you. Sit down, sit down." He motioned toward two chairs in front of his desk and I plunked down in one of them. He sat back down.

"My salesperson says you already own on the beach. That so?"

"Yes, I do."

"Where abouts?"

I decided to throw a little weight around. "The Island."

His eyes sparkled. "Yes, yes. Prime property. Like to sell?"

"No, Mr. Norris. Not unless I have to someday."

He seemed disappointed as the potential commission slipped away like a steamed clam down a drunk's throat.

"Yeah, yeah. I can't blame you. And it's Ted. So anyway, what can I do for you, Mr...?"

"Marlowe. And it's Dan."

"Well, Mr. Marlowe, what can I do for you?"

"Well, Ted. I'd like to ask you about a family friend, Cora Sweeney."

He sat up in his chair. "Cora Sweeney, Cora Sweeney. Hmmm. The woman that killed herself down on Reed Street. A real tragedy. My condolences, Mr. Marlowe."

"Thanks." Even though I already knew the answer, I was curious how he'd play it. "Were you her landlord?"

He didn't answer right away, just stared at me, and I wondered for a moment if he was going to lie. "Yes, yes. I was the poor woman's landlord."

I decided to hold my ace question until last. "She was a good tenant?"

"The best. Especially considering what can sometimes happen around here. You've probably been on the beach awhile, so you might know. The stories I could tell you about what renters pull. I had someone once who had a horse living in the cottage with them. A damn horse! The worst part was when I confronted them and told them to get rid of it, they thought I was being unreasonable. Can you believe that?"

I almost couldn't. And here I thought I'd heard every rental horror story there was on this beach, but I'd never heard one about a horse before.

"Anyhow, I finally got them and the horse out of there. And did that place smell! Jesus H. Christ. It's never smelled the same since. I've lost plenty of rentals 'cause of that odor. Mrs. Sweeney was a dream compared to what I've had to deal with in the past. Of course, she was in a wheelchair so there couldn't be too many wild parties or anything."

These real estate people all have the gift of gab, it's their stock in trade, so I figured I'd better ask my important question before he got going on something else, like maybe an elephant in a motel room. "Was Cora a year-round or a winter rental?"

His expression changed for just an instant and then smoothed back out into Mr. Real Estate. The look came and went so fast I couldn't tell what it meant. After a long silence he said, "She was a year-round rental. When she first moved in I decided to help her out by giving her a yearly. Being in a wheelchair and all."

"That was nice of you."

"As you know, we're all like one big family here in Happy Hampton Beach, Mr. Marlowe."

Sure we were. I decided to throw this philanthropist a little white lie. "Someone told me you were trying to get her out before summer this year."

I could see the man actually bristle and he became defensive. "Well, well, I didn't want to, but if you know the beach, Mr. Marlowe, you know last year was a bad year economics-wise here. I asked Mrs. Sweeney if she'd consider leaving for the summer. I would've given her a few bucks, of course. I'll admit I could've used the extra income I would've received for a summer rental. But she was having none of it and that was the end of it."

"The end of it?"

His eyes narrowed and he answered, "Yes, Mr. Marlowe, the end of it."

I stood up. "Okay, Mr...ahh...Ted. I want to thank you for your time."

He jumped up. For a minute I thought he was going to ask me some questions; instead, he reached across the desk and pumped my hand again. "Anytime, anytime, Mr. Marlowe. Goodbye."

I left his office and walked past the saleswoman who nodded like her head was as heavy as one of the boulders down at the jetty. Outside, I got hit with a blast of salt air and it smelled damn good. Refreshing. I kept smelling that salt air all the way back to my cottage at the other end of the beach.

The air seemed to sharpen my mind and actually helped give me a couple of good ideas about what I had learned from Ted Norris. But what the hell it all added up to, I still didn't know.

Chapter 14

I DIDN'T GET MUCH ELSE accomplished the rest of the day, and by ten o'clock that night I was ready to hit the hay. I'd just polished off my one and only Heineken for the night and clicked off the TV when I heard footsteps coming up the front porch stairs. I didn't get overly anxious—living at the beach you learn that anyone's liable to show up at your door at any time. It's not suburbia. When I heard a double knock at the door, I didn't get up to answer it, just asked who was there.

"Ahhh, for the love a Jaysus, Danny, it's me."

I got up and opened the door and there stood the Irishman, in his restaurant whites as usual. Shamrock didn't make a habit of coming by my cottage this late, so I was a little surprised to see him but not disappointed. He was one of only a few people I didn't mind seeing outside the work environment.

I almost asked if he wanted a beer before I realized what a foolish question that would've been. I got Shamrock his beer, another for me. When I came back into the front room he was staring at a framed photograph I had hanging on the wall. It's an aerial photo of Hampton Beach, and if you study it closely, you can actually make out every cottage and building on the beach.

"Let's see now." He was running his finger over the picture, trying to locate something. "There she is."

I handed him his Heineken and looked over his shoulder. He was pointing at one of the back streets off Ashworth. "That's my place," Shamrock said.

We clinked our bottles together. He smiled and took a long swig. I glanced again at where he'd pointed on the photograph. It was only a street over from where Cora Sweeney had lived.

Shamrock settled down on the old couch and I sat back in my chair. My comfortable chair. Matter of fact, everything in the cottage was comfortable. Inexpensive, but very comfortable. And clean too. There were three small bedrooms, a kitchen, one bathroom, and the front room Shamrock and I were sitting in now. For a beach place my little cottage was definitely above average. And I was keeping the place in pretty good shape, too, for a guy all alone. Giving it my best shot, trying not to let the cottage—or me—go to seed. Of course, two of the bedrooms didn't need much attention anymore; the kids hadn't used them in quite a while.

I flicked the TV back on and we drank our beer. For a few minutes I thought that Shamrock had dropped by just to shoot the shit. But I was hoping it was more than that.

"Danny," he said finally, holding the empty Heineken in front of him as if he were proposing a toast. "I been talking to some people like you asked me, and I heard somethin' you might be interested in."

"What did you hear?"

"Well, it's only talk, Danny. Just talk. And it doesn't matter who it came from, does it?" He looked at me with those round blue eyes, and I figured he wanted some re-assurance that he was right—that it didn't matter to me who'd told him whatever the hell he was going to tell me. I knew where Shamrock had probably gotten his informa-tion—either from a neighbor of his and Cora's, or a High Tide worker, or maybe a barfly at The Crooked Shillelagh. The man rarely went anywhere else.

I didn't feel like playing games at this hour, but Sham-rock and I'd been through a lot together. "No, I don't care who you heard it from. Now what the hell did you hear?"

Shamrock straightened up on the sofa and looked around as if he thought someone might be listening. He even lowered his voice. "It's about Cora Sweeney. I found somethin' out and it ain't nice."

"What is it?"

"You know Frankie's T-shirt Shop?"

I had to think for a minute. There were so many T-shirt shops on the beach I often wondered how they could all make money. There was one shop that came to mind. "The one run by the guy with the big earring?"

Shamrock bobbed his head. "Yes, that's him. That's why they call him Frankie Earring. Well, he's no good."

"What did he do?"

Shamrock held his empty green Heineken bottle over his head and jiggled it. So I went to the kitchen and got us two more beers. When I returned Shamrock was as jumpy as a barefooted man on a hot July sidewalk.

He leaned in closer to me. "You see this Frankie Earring...the bastard...he has kids stealing for him. Breaking into cottages and stores. Even stealing watches and cameras and wallets right off the beach in the summer."

I hadn't heard this before and it was interesting, but still..."What's that got to do with Cora Sweeney?"

"Well," Shamrock began before stopping and draining half the new Heineken I'd given him. "I heard he had her boy stealing for him. And that she heard about it and threatened to turn Frankie into the cops."

Now that was interesting, very interesting. Someone else with a motive for wanting to see Cora Sweeney go bye-bye. "Did she?" I asked.

Shamrock held up a hand like he was stopping traffic. "I don't know, but she told half the beach she was going to. That's what I heard, Danny. I thought it might be important. Is it, Danny boy? Is it important?"

Now that was the million dollar question. I shook my head. "I don't know, Shamrock. Thanks for looking into it though."

He gave a dismissive wave. "It was nothing. I feel bad for that young lad running around the beach. I hope this'll help him."

I wasn't sure it would, but I didn't tell Shamrock that. He had a good heart and I wanted him to believe he was helping. Then I remembered something. "You know anything about Cora's landlord, Beautiful Beach Real Estate?"

"Just a regular real estate business, I guess. Why? Something wrong?"

"No, I don't think so."

"I'll see what else I can dig up, Danny."

Shamrock had done enough and besides I didn't want him to get in any more trouble than he might already be in. "No, Shamrock. That's plenty. Thanks."

He became animated. "No, no, no. I won't hear of such a thing. I want to help you and the boy."

I knew better than to try and argue with an Irishman when he had his mind set. Besides, I owed Shamrock. And I trusted him. But I couldn't let anything happen to him either. If it did, it'd be my fault.

"All right. But after what happened at the Tide the other morning, we've got to be more careful. We can't talk about it there—too many ears. And I don't want anyone following you down here. They'll know you're poking around."

Shamrock rubbed his freckled chin, then snapped his fingers. "I got it. We meet somewhere else. Somewhere out in the open, so we'd see if we was followed."

"Okay. That could work." At least it was better than meeting here.

"But where?" Shamrock said, looking around the room as if he expected the answer to be on a wall.

I knew the answer instantly. "The jetty."

The jetty was only about a hundred yards from my cottage at the extreme south end of the beach. The boulder formation jutted out into the Atlantic and formed a breakwater protecting Hampton Harbor. In season, tourists loved to walk the length of its flat-topped rocks out to the end and back. But now, in May, that area of the beach would be deserted most nights. It was secluded and barren. It'd be tough for anyone to follow Shamrock there or sneak up on us while we were talking.

"Ahh, the jetty. That's smart. But when?"

"You can let me know if you get any new info. Discreetly at the Tide or call me here at the cottage. Then we can set up a time to meet."

Shamrock nodded. "Good, good," he said. He was staring at the empty beer bottle in his fist. If he squeezed any harder, I'd be picking green shards of glass off the floor for the next hour

Even though I didn't really want to drink anymore, I couldn't very well yawn in Shamrock's face and toss him out. "Can you stay for another beer?"

"Is the Pope Catholic?" he answered, a big grin spreading across that Irish mug of his.

I got up and got us more beer. Needless to say, it was another long night.

Chapter 15

I DIDN'T FEEL SO HOT the next morning. I was jittery and my mouth tasted foul. Don't ever try to keep pace drinking with an Irishman. At least not one who came over on the boat. Even though I felt dead bad, it was time to get moving. I had to check out Frankie Earring. Find out what the hell was going on with him.

And somehow I had to find Kelsey. Christ, the kid had been out sleeping under cottages and — I hoped — somehow finding enough to eat for almost a week now.

Besides, I had to keep that promise I'd made to myself, no matter how anxious I was feeling.

By the time I reached my destination it was almost nine-thirty, with a half-hour left before I had to be at the Tide. It was a cloudy Tuesday, which was okay with me. When you lived at the beach year-round you got so much sun that cloudy days were a nice break. As long as it didn't end up raining—at the beach that's the worst.

Ocean Boulevard wasn't crowded, it was still the week before Memorial Day. I stood on the sidewalk staring at Frankie's T-Shirt Shop. The shop was sandwiched between a fried dough stand and a beachwear store and had T-shirts plastered on both sides of the entrance with slogans like *Silly Faggot, Dicks are for Chicks* printed on them.

Now what kind of hammerhead would wear that? I wondered. But I couldn't wonder for long. I'd come here for a reason. Might as well get to it.

The front of the shop had one of those large overhead doors you see on a garage like a lot of retail businesses on the beach did. The door was swung up so the entire front of the store was open. There were racks and racks of T-shirts with a long glass display case along one side of the store. On top of the case sat a cash register and a heat transfer machine for applying design transfers to the shirts. There were only a couple of customers squeezing their way between the racks. Behind the display case stood the proprietor, Frankie Earring.

The large gold hoop earring he wore in his left ear gave him away. I'd seen this character floating around the beach for years. The beach is like that. A lot of familiar faces drift up and down Ocean Boulevard and even hang out at specific stores. Oftentimes the locals don't have any idea what their real game is. Like with me and this Frankie Earring guy. Sure, I'd seen him in front of his joint lots of times, but until Shamrock had mentioned him, I hadn't known if he was an owner, worker, or hanger-outer. Hell, I hadn't been in a T-shirt shop in 15 years. Why should I have been? They're all the same and they're for the tourists, anyway.

I screwed up my courage, walked into the shop, and marched up to the display case. Frankie Earring was bent over punching some figures into a handheld calculator. He didn't look up and I noticed the brown hair he had slicked back and tied into a small ponytail was thin on top. Why do a lot of guys with thin hair have ponytails anyway? And why have long hair if you're just going to put it in a ponytail?

"I'm hoping you can help me," I said.

Frankie stood full up and looked at me as if I was intruding. That was the first thing I noticed. The second was his size. He was a big one. At least four inches taller than me and muscular. He had on a T-shirt that said, *Do Not Disturb – I'm Disturbed Enough Already.*

When he spoke, I got another surprise. "Yeth, maybe I can," he said with a pronounced lisp.

Instantly I felt more confident. "I'm here about a young boy." I realized how odd that sounded the second I'd said it, so I quickly added, "His name is Kelsey Sweeney. Do you know him?"

I could tell the wheels were spinning behind Frankie Earring's brown eyes. "The name thounds familiar," he answered. His tongue flicked across his lips.

That emboldened me further. "It should sound familiar. I heard that you had a run-in with his mother a while ago."

Frankie tapped the silver skull ring on his right hand against the glass display case top. "Who are you? A cop?"

"I'm a friend of the family. And the word on the beach is you had some hot words with the lady. They say you were using the boy to pull rip-offs and she threatened to sic the cops on you if you didn't lay off her son. Am I right so far?"

Frankie Earring glanced around furtively. He'd probably prefer to move this talk into the back room but he was alone in the store. Leave a business unattended on the beach for more than a couple of minutes and kids would strip it clean. "I didn't have anything to do with her kid breaking in platheths. I tried to tell her that. She wouldn't believe me."

"I wonder why," I said. "Like I said, the word's out all over the beach, Frankie. You're using kids for rip-offs. Cora Sweeney threatened you with the cops, and before you can zoom down the Waterslide she's dead."

He turned pale and shook his head vigorously. "She OD'd, didn't she?"

"Maybe, maybe not," I said.

Frankie became more hyper. "Look, no matter how she died, I didn't have anything to do with it. Even if what she wath ranting and raving about wath true, which I'm not thaying it wath, I wouldn't have any reason to kill her. Not for one louthy kid breaking in cottages."

I leaned into him. "Speaking of the kid, Frankie. I don't want to see anything even close to what happened to his mother happening to him."

"Are you kidding? I hope I never thee that kid again. Nothing but trouble." Then his eyes raked over my face. He jutted his chin at me and said, "You're the bartender down at the High Tide, aren't you?"

Almost everyone connected with this thing, guilty or innocent, probably knew who I was by now. No sense trying to conceal it. Made me stop and think, though. Everyone knew who I was but did I really know who any of them were?

"Doesn't matter who I am, Frankie. We're talking about you using kids to pull your little scores."

He suddenly got defensive. "I told you what I know and I'm not talking anymore. Now leave my thtore."

"Sure, Frankie," I said before turning to leave. "Just remember though. Anything happens to that boy, someone's going to pay."

Back out on Ocean Boulevard I suddenly got the shakes. I had no idea what I'd accomplished with Frankie Earring except maybe to scare him off hurting Kelsey. If what Shamrock had told me about Frankie's little side business was true, then he was one of the sleaziest characters I'd met on the beach so far. Not all sleazy characters were murderers, though, were they?

Lost in thought, I almost banged into someone heading the opposite way. I mumbled an apology but he was past me like a greyhound. I turned and recognized the shiny bald head of the Chamber of Commerce guy hot-footing along the boulevard. That was a good thing. The man usually wasn't spotted on the beach until preparations for the summer season were under way. Kind of like that groundhog thing. So at least something positive had come out of this little excursion—a sign that summer was right around the corner.

Chapter 16

I THOUGHT IT WAS GOING to be just another day behind the bar at the High Tide. I came in, set the bar up like I did every morning, did a little bullshitting with the kitchen people, read my newspapers, and waited for the lunch crowd. The waitresses were puttering around over in the dining area, putting their stations in order for the noon rush. A couple of regulars came in, sat at the end of the bar, and I busied myself serving them.

It was about 11 a.m. when things suddenly changed. The front door flew open and into the bar stormed trouble. She was thin as a rail, wore black boots, a Harley T-shirt, and jeans. Her long black hair was streaked with grey and hadn't been washed recently. Tattoos decorated both arms. She might have been about my age, but I couldn't be sure; she had a lot of hard living etched onto her face.

She plunked herself down on a stool at the middle of the bar and stared daggers at me. I walked over and started to ask if she wanted a menu.

"I don't want nothin'. You Marlowe?"

"Yeah," I said warily.

"I'm Mona Freeman and I'm here to tell ya to keep away from my man."

I didn't know what she meant, but she was loud and threatening and if she'd been a guy and had a few more pounds on her, I probably would've been more worried than I was.

"You bother him once more and I got friends that'll kick your young ass from here to the bridge and back."

I liked the young part—the rest, not so much. I stayed a good arm's length away from her. After all, there was glassware on the bar. "I don't know what the heck you're talking about," I said. I could see out of the corner of my eye that the two regulars at the end of the bar were enjoying the show.

She shouted at me, spittle flying, and I noticed her teeth were bad. "Like hell you don't. You been hasslin' my man. Ober Sweeney. And if you come around him again, you're gonna get your ass beat."

I should've guessed. Now that I looked more closely at her, I could see she actually resembled Sweeney a bit. I tried a reasonable tack. "I wasn't there hassling him. I was there to tell him about his son."

"Yeah and to ask him where he was the night that cripple whore killed herself. Why you askin' him questions like that? You tryin' to get him in trouble?"

I stared at her face, pinched and red. She looked about ready to come across the bar at me. I glanced under the sink at the Georgia toothpick we kept for such purposes, but realized I couldn't use a baseball bat on a woman, even one like this. Unless maybe she pulled a knife.

"I went to see him to tell him about his son," I repeated. "The boy's on the beach with nowhere to live."

"That ain't O and me's problem. O's been sending that bitch money for the kid for years. And that's money me and him could of used." She raised her voice even louder. "So I don't want you fuckin' bothering him again."

I noticed the two regulars at the end of the bar had stopped enjoying the show and were looking more uncomfortable by the minute. I held up my hands like I was telling traffic to slow down. "Look, keep it down or get the hell out of here. There's the door right behind you."

A familiar tic started under her left eye. "I know where I came in. But you got a nerve coming to my house and accusing my man of being involved in that freakin' slut's death. The only times he ever went over there is when she called and begged him to come over so she could get some money for that punk kid a their's. And I finally put my foot down with those little trips, too. Don't know why you're buttin' in, anyhow. You ain't no cop and the silly tramp killed herself anyway."

"That's what the police say. They've been wrong before." I had one more thing on my mind, the kind of question that just might bring her over the bar. What the hell. If she got more belligerent then she already was, I could always call the cops. "And obviously you and Ober didn't like paying that child support, did you?"

"What are you saying, that O'd kill her for the crummy child support payments he was making? The whore and the kid didn't deserve it, but O wouldn't waste his time hurting her over chump change."

Now I was getting somewhere. "What about if you added in the money from the accident settlement? The money the court ordered him to pay back? Would you or Ohhh waste your time over an amount like that?"

The fact that I knew about the accident money Sweeney had stolen from his ex-wife and had been ordered to pay back in hefty installments by the court surprised her. But she came back quick and started banging her fist hard on the bar. Her fingers had burn marks and her skin was dry and deeply cracked. She also could've used that stuff mothers put on kid's fingernails to stop them from chewing their fingers to nubs.

"You stay away from him and from our place. Or you'll be one sorry fuck." She got up from her stool and stomped out of the bar. I stared as her Harley-Davidson T-shirt disappeared through the front door.

I freshened the drinks for my two customers, who both tried to pretend nothing unusual had just happened. Something I couldn't do. My hands shook and my breath came in short little gasps. I touched the prescription bottle in the front pocket of my jeans and focused on calming down.

Looked like I'd stumbled into another hornet's nest. But I had found out some interesting bits of information. One, that this Mona Freeman had a hot temper and a couple of good reasons to want Cora Sweeney out of the picture permanently—namely, jealousy and greed. And two, that I'd better watch my back—she was the type who just might have some unpleasant friends of hers visit me like she'd threatened.

Good thing the lunch gang started to file in just then and kept me from over thinking what had just happened. I'd calmed down a bit and proceeded to lose myself in the work. The rest of the shift was uneventful, except for one thing—Shamrock buttonholed me and said we should get together later that night. I hadn't expected him to have anything that quick so I figured whatever he had must be important. We agreed to meet at the jetty at ten.

Chapter 17

TEN O'CLOCK CAME SLOW but eventually I looked up at the anchor-shaped clock on my cottage wall and found that my scheduled meeting time with Shamrock at the jetty was only ten minutes away. I grabbed a lightweight jacket and headed out the door.

It was a beautiful night. Clear sky and stars you just can't see in the big city. After I got over the dunes, I headed south along the beach in the direction of the jetty. The moon was almost full and it lit up the ocean like something you would see in a travel brochure. The tide was about halfway to high and the waves in the moonlight rolled gently against the shore.

I glanced back over my shoulder and noticed a few scattered figures along the beach, way up somewhere near the Casino. But on this end I was the lone walker. Too late at night and too early in the season for other people to be about. Shamrock and I had been right about the privacy we'd be afforded. The air was a little cool and I was glad I'd worn a jacket.

Up ahead I could see the dark outline of the jetty and beyond it a sprinkling of lights, homes across the water in Seabrook. I couldn't tell if Shamrock was there yet. I hoped this meeting wasn't just some silly Shamrock thing. The Irishman was a great guy and he'd give you his last beer, but sometimes he'd do something and I'd find myself wondering if he'd had a bit too much Guinness in him. And believe me that'd have to be a lot; his capacity was legendary on the beach.

As I drew closer to the jetty I couldn't see any sign of my friend. I scanned the length of the rock outcrop that wasn't already concealed by the incoming tide. Nothing...except way out near the tip of the jetty, close to the twenty-foot tall reflector pole that warned boats away from the rocks. From here I could see something flopping around, half in and half out of the water. Each new wave would conceal the white object for a moment, then it would pop into view again. I got a sick feeling in my stomach and sprinted the last few yard to the rocks.

Even though there's a thick steel cable to hang onto running the length of the jetty, it's still suicide to try to run on the rocks. The stacked boulders hide deep crevices and are slippery as hell when wet.

Wet or not didn't matter. Not if what I suspected was true.

I jumped up on the closest rock, took a few quick steps, and lost my footing right away. I grabbed the cable just in time to avoid a nasty fall, then kept hold of the cold, wet steel as I scrambled over the giant rocks. Out here, the moonlight was deceiving, highlighting the surface just enough to bolster my confidence. Couldn't see much beyond the tops of the rocks and the water, though. Luckily I got a glimpse of a few spots where there were chasms between the boulders and without stopping I'd make a leap. A couple of times I'd skid or trip but somehow I didn't go down and I kept moving.

I glanced at the object ahead. Whatever I'd seen bobbing on the waves was still there. Every so often a wave would wash over it and it would disappear for a second, only to come into view again before the next wave hit.

By the time I reached the end of the jetty the water was up to my thighs, and I realized the sick feeling in my gut had been right: the object I'd been focused on was Shamrock. He was in chest-deep water.

"Shamrock, what the fuck?"

Shamrock didn't say a word. His bare head lolled to one side and his eyes were unfocused. There was a thin stream of blood cutting his forehead in half. I grabbed his shoulders and shook hard. "Shamrock!"

His blue eyes cleared a bit and focused on me. "Danny. Mother of God, it's you. Help me."

I put one arm under his shoulder and tried to lift. He groaned and let out a hiss of pain.

"They got my foot jammed in down there."

An incoming wave washed over him, splashing me in the face. He coughed and spit out sea water as the wave receded. I wished I'd taken some time through the years to study the tides: how fast was the water coming in and how high was it likely to get?

I couldn't see a thing under the water's surface. I eased down beside Shamrock and reached into the dark water. I slid my hand along his pant leg, trying to find what was holding him down. No luck. I swallowed, held my breath, and sank beneath the ocean's surface.

While the moonlight brightened the above-water world, underneath the water that same brightness was only a dull glow. I ran my hand down Shamrock's leg again—and ran into a slimy boulder. I came up for air.

"Danny, sweet Jaysus. Get me outta here. The water's coming up fast."

He was right. Every wave was bigger than the last and when the wave receded, a little less of his body was left above the water. I ducked back into the water, felt around till I had his calf, and pulled.

Even through the water I could hear Shamrock's groan.

I came up quick, took one look at his rolling eyes, and grabbed him. "Shamrock, look at me. Shamrock."

He blinked and said softly, like he'd just about given up. "Danny boy. Please."

No way was I going to let this happen. I'd lost almost everything. I wasn't going to lose Shamrock too. And all because he'd asked a few questions. For me.

I sucked in a lungful of salty air and went under face first. I stretched out on the rocks so I was on my belly. I reached both arms into the crevice, ran my hand down the length of Shamrock's calf until I reached his ankle. I almost lost it when my hand ran into an object that could only be a bone poking against Shamrock's pants. No wonder he'd been moaning when I pulled. My lungs screamed as I ran my hands down in the narrowing crevice. Finally, I found his sneaker, solidly jammed on all sides. I gave a slight tug on the foot, trying not to think about Shamrock's reaction. The foot didn't move.

I had to have air and rose out of the water, coughing and gasping. Shamrock was out cold, chin resting on his white shirt. Another wave washed over us and when the ocean receded this time, water lapped against his lower lip. His time—our time—had run out.

I sucked air again, threw myself back under water, stretched out on my belly, and dropped my arms back into the hole that held Shamrock's leg. There were only two possibilities and solution number two was out of the question. So I went for number one and hoped Shamrock's Irish luck would hold out.

I ran my hand carefully over the protrusion near his ankle, felt around the top of the sneaker, found the shoelace, and pulled the shoelace loose. Fumbling blindly, I loosened the lace from the eyes just like you might if you were taking off a tight-fitting shoe, then stuck my fingers down into the sneaker and around the bottom of

Shamrock's foot. Wedging my other hand down into the same space, I grabbed hold of Shamrock's calf as close to the ankle as I could get without pushing on what I now was certain was a protruding bone, and pulled.

For a minute I didn't think my grand solution was going to work. I pulled harder, fighting the rocks, the water, the screaming of my lungs, and suddenly Shamrock's foot slipped out of the sneaker and he was free.

I got my feet back under me and stood up gasping. I grabbed Shamrock under both shoulders and pulled him up against me. His eyelids fluttered and I heaved a sigh of relief. He wasn't fully conscious, but he was alive.

I've walked the length of that jetty dozens of times in my life, carried my exhausted toddlers from one end to the other, but that night's trek was the longest by far. When Shamrock came to, he tried to help, but I supported him the whole way, somehow getting the two of us over every chasm and rocky obstacle.

We didn't say much or talk about how he'd ended up out there; there'd be time for that later. I did ask him how his ankle was.

"Broken," he said.

I'd known that already.

Other than that my talkative Irish friend didn't say much on the slog back to the beach. When we hit the sand, he finally spoke up. "Danny, my boy. I wasn't worried one bit. I knew you'd get me outta there as sure as there's a Blarney Stone in Ireland. You're the best friend a man could have.

Then he added, "Would you mind going back for my sneaker?"

Chapter 18

"I GUESS YOU WON'T NEED that sneaker after all," I said. It was the next morning. I'd lied my way into Shamrock's room at the hospital in Exeter, New Hampshire by claiming to be his brother. I'd done it once before; it'd worked then, too. I sat on a chair beside his bed and studied him. He certainly looked a lot better than the last time I'd seen him here. That'd been after I'd pulled him half-frozen out of the ice machine at the High Tide. I shook my head, trying to dislodge that unpleasant memory.

"Very good, Danny boy. You're getting better with age." Shamrock was propped up in the bed, pillow behind his back. As usual, he was all in white, but this time a hospital johnny covered him instead of his normal work whites. All the way from the neck down to the sheet that covered the rest of his body. I noticed a gauze bandage covering a small section on the top of his head where, according to Shamrock, his attackers had whacked him with a gun. Otherwise, he looked normal.

"I'm learning from the best," I said and I meant it. "How you feeling?"

"All right, I guess. The doc says they'll be doing the job on my ankle this afternoon. My noggin's fine. A mild concussion, a few stitches."

"Good. How long will you be in here?"

"They didn't say, Danny. You can bet yer last pound it won't be long. They'd throw out Saint Patrick as fast as they could even if he was handin' out free tickets to Heaven."

I glanced at the other bed in the room—empty and made up. "That's the truth. It's all about insurance. By the way, you all set?"

"I think that crappy...ahh...that policy from the Tide'll cover most of it." Shamrock's face turned red which was unusual. He could go back and forth with the best of them and was rarely caught embarrassed.

I waved my hand. "Don't worry about it, Shamrock. I was lucky I kept that policy in force when the Tide started going under. It was all I could swing. I even let my own expire. Dianne just hasn't gotten a chance to update the policy yet."

"I know. And I love Dianne but you know the restaurant business—it's built on cheap wages and cheaper benefits. I tried to talk about that with the boys once back home but even they didn't like that talk. Tossed my Irish ass out on the cold wet streets of Derry."

I knew who the "boys" were but rarely did Shamrock talk about that phase of his life. I wondered if he was over medicated. "Well, if there's money or anything else I can do to help, just ask." And I meant that too.

Shamrock fiddled with the drip tube going into his arm. "I know, Danny. I'm fine."

I got down to business. "So what the hell happened?"

Shamrock straightened the front of his johnny. "It was my own stupidity. They followed me, I guess. But I didn't see the pair of 'em 'til I got to the state park. You know, all open like it is. They'd probably been with me since I left my place but I hadn't seen 'em. If I had, you can be sure they never would have got their mitts on Michael Kelly. When I first saw 'em, I just thought that they were a couple of winter stew bums. Boy, was I wrong."

"Did you see who they were?"

"Masks, Danny. Just like your visitor in the kitchen. I did notice something though. One of 'em had a bandaged right paw. Suspicious, don't ya think?"

"Yeah, I think," I answered. I didn't believe in coincidences and every word Shamrock uttered told me we were in a lot deeper trouble than I'd ever intended. "And then?"

Shamrock turned his hands up. "Then I lost sight of 'em when I went over the dunes and headed for the jetty. Next time I saw the no-goods I'd just reached the rocks and they was jammin' a gun in my back, tellin' me I been diggin' around where I shouldn't."

"They mention anybody, Shamrock?"

He pointed his finger at me. "Just you, Danny. Said the whole thing was your fault. The liars. I knew what I was gettin' into. And I'd do it again." Shamrock nodded his head. "Yes, surely I would. It ain't easy to scare Michael Kelly. Anyhow, they said we'd had enough chances. That's when one a them said he had an idea and they walked me out on the jetty where you found me. Bastards jammed my foot down between those rocks and gave me a little love tap with the gun on my squash. Worse, they was laughing as they walked away. I'm tellin' ya, Danny boy, I thought I was a goner 'til you showed up. I tried to get my foot loose, but every time I lowered my head it hurt so much I'd almost pass out. I was afraid if I did, I'd drown. Even when I saw you, I still didn't know if I was ever gonna see the old sod again. You saved my life. Again. I owe ya."

"You've done that and more for me through the years, Shamrock." And the man had. Back when almost every sane person on the beach had given up on me.

His face turned red again. I changed the subject to the one important thing left. "Why did you want to meet at the jetty anyway?"

The red left his cheeks. "Jaysus, that was the oddest thing. I got a call saying you and I ought to check out Cora Sweeney's cottage. That there were things going on at the beach we didn't know nothin' about. And the answers might be there."

"Did you recognize the voice?"

"No, but it sounded like me mother without the brogue."

"An old woman? And she mentioned me by name?"

"Yes. She said 'you and Dan Marlowe'." Shamrock glanced up at the overhanging television. "I wonder what ya gotta do around here to get that thing turned on?"

"I'll take care of it before I leave."

"Thank you, Danny. They're lucky it's not Sunday. There's Irish step-dancing on Sunday mornings. They'd really see an Irish temper if I missed that. Anyhow, I think I screwed up a little."

"Why?" I asked. I adjusted my position in the uncomfortable chair.

Shamrock looked away. "I called up that damn Beautiful Beach place you said was her landlord. I thought I'd just pretend that I was a renter. You know how these beach agents let you take the key on your own sometimes, check the place out. I was hoping to do that, then I could search around the cottage alone, see if the call meant anything."

"Who'd you talk to?"

"The secretary put me right through to a guy. Maybe the owner. I dunno. Anyhow, he shot the whole idea down. Said the place wasn't for rent. Maybe I got a little hot. He hung up on me. Not too good a move—huh, Danny?"

No, it wasn't. But I wasn't going to say that to Shamrock. The poor guy had been through enough. Besides, it didn't make any difference now. I didn't bother asking if he'd used a fake name. His accent might have given him away anyhow.

"It could've been how you got the tails." But I wasn't sure. Like I said before, this kind of stuff was all new to me.

Shamrock brightened up. "So that's why I wanted to meet. I was figuring you'd want to know about the old woman's call."

I nodded. "You did good, Shamrock."

"So whatta we do now?"

I was just about to tell him I had absolutely no idea when a pretty young nurse strolled in. "Good morning, Mr. Kelly. How are we feeling this morning?"

Shamrock jumped right in with his Irish charm. That man could talk a monkey into giving him his last banana. "I'd feel a lot better if a bonnie lassie like you would call me Michael."

"I guess you're feeling just fine then."

I've learned through the years that most nurses are good with banter—they have to be in their job. I've never met one that could outdo Shamrock Kelly though. The two went back and forth as she opened a small box she'd brought in with her. She removed a hypodermic needle with syringe and inserted it into the tube running into Shamrock's arm.

"Hey, Danny," Shamrock said. "Here comes the good stuff."

Yeah, the good stuff. The kind of stuff that made me uneasy. "I'm going to go now, Shamrock. I'll be back."

"Okay. But don't do anything 'til they spring me from this place. It's too dangerous. You'll need me."

"All right." But I wasn't sure I was going to keep that promise. I got up, nodded goodbye to the pretty nurse, and tried not to stare as she withdrew the hypodermic needle from the tube.

Chapter 19

I WAS JUST A COUPLE of miles from the beach when I heard the explosion. For a minute I thought the Seabrook Nuclear Power Plant had popped its cork. Like a lot of beach people I'd had that possibility in the back of my mind since they'd built the damn thing. Although I'd always figured if the plant went big time, I wouldn't be alive to hear it. On the other hand, if there was a smaller explosion that caused a leak, that could be trouble. I wondered if I should stop while I could and avoid the traffic jam trying to get off the beach before a radioactive cloud descended.

I didn't have to make a decision. Ahead of me a thin black cloud of smoke rose over Hampton Beach. I couldn't tell exactly where it was but it had to be somewhere in the beach district proper. I drove faster. I could hear sirens already.

By the time I got to Ashworth Avenue, the police already had part of the road blocked off. I drove as far as I could and parked near Royal Market. I got out and fast-walked in the direction of the smoke. I could see fire trucks and a lot of human activity and knew they were on Reed Street. My stomach churned like I'd eaten a bad clam.

I had to slow down when I rounded the corner of Reed. The street was littered with chunks of wood and glass, some still smoldering. I stepped over the fire hoses criss-crossing the street and maneuvered around pools of water. Locals, some still in their pajamas, were lined up on the far side of the street. They were chattering to each other—some pointed at the destruction, others covered their mouths and shook their heads. I hurried along the line of people until I spotted Steve Moore. He was decked out in his tie and gun and didn't look very happy. I stopped beside him and didn't say anything. He looked straight ahead, staring at the same thing everyone else was staring at. So I stared along with him. Wasn't hard to see what had gotten the crowd's attention. Cora Sweeney's cottage. What was left of it.

Firemen worked their hoses up and down the entire area. The beach has a history of fires gone wild. All this water had to be about preventing the fire from leaping onto someone else's cottage, because there was definitely nothing left to burn at Cora's. All that was left of Cora's place was a smoking pile of ash and blackened wood. Half a dozen or so stacks of soot-smeared concrete blocks that must've each been a few feet high, poked out of the rubble here and there. It took me a minute to recognize that they were the foundation that'd kept the building off the ground. The fire chief paced up and down in front of the rubble, barking orders to his men. A photographer with an expensive-looking rig snapped photos, sprinting around to get shots from different angles. The one-story cottages on both sides of Cora's had their windows blown out and the sides of the buildings were badly damaged. The siding on one appeared to have melted. The insurance agents who handled the beach were definitely going to be busy.

"What the hell happened, Steve?" I finally asked.

He turned, noticed me for the first time, then turned back to look at the scene. "How the hell would I know? I just got here."

"Gas?"

He didn't answer my question. "How's Kelly?"

I wasn't surprised he knew about that; a report had been made after all. But I was hoping somehow he hadn't heard about the incident. "I was just over at Exeter. He's doing ok. They're going to fix the ankle this afternoon."

"Didn't I ask you to stop poking around the beach?"

His voice was flat, so flat I couldn't tell if he was pissed off. I glanced at his face but couldn't see anything but sunglasses and a stony expression. I looked back at the smoky ruin. "That's what I've been trying to do," I lied again.

"That's bullshit." The way he said it left no doubt in my mind: he was angry. And not just a little bit. "You've still been making your rounds on the beach like you're Sherlock Holmes or something. And now you've almost got your Dr. Watson, the poor stupe Kelly, killed. If he'd ended up dead, it'd be your damn fault."

He was right about that. Probably wouldn't make him any less angry if I told him I felt like a piece of shit about it, either. So instead, I said, "How'd you know about...my rounds, Steve?"

He answered me like I was just another dumb civilian. "There's things going on around here you aren't privy to. There are people and things we're watching that have nothing to do with Cora Sweeney's death. You just keep popping up on the radar. And we want you off it."

So that was it. The cops had their eye on somebody or somebodies. But who? Ted Norris? Frankie Earring? Mona Freeman? Shamrock? Or maybe even me?

I wasn't going to quit so I had only one way to go. "Look, Steve, I made a promise to Kelsey that I'd check into this thing and I'm not going to stop. I think he's right about his mother being killed. There's just too much going on here."

Steve and I both watched as two fire engines—one from Seabrook, the other from Rye—pulled to the head of the street from different directions on Ashworth. They added to the clutter of those that were already there. The Hampton chief waved the new arrivals into position. I didn't see how they could help at this point.

"You're asking for trouble, Dan," Steve said. I was surprised when he added, "But I guess it's your life."

"Yeah," I said warily. Then I nodded at the mess across the street. "What about this?"

"I thought gas was your deduction, Sherlock?"

I didn't like the joke but I wasn't going to start trouble either. I had enough of that. "What else could level a house like that?"

"Well..." Steve began just as his name was shouted by a fireman up at the head of Reed Street. The man waved. "I gotta see what he wants. I'll see you later. And try to stay out of this. Remember what I told you."

I watched Steve's back as he walked away. No way I was going to stay out of anything and I'd already forgotten most of what he'd told me. At least everything that was of no use in figuring out what the hell was going on here and who exactly was behind it. I scanned the debris-littered lot that used to be Cora and Kelsey Sweeney's home. Someone, maybe Ted Norris, would probably try to squeeze as many cheap condos onto that lot as he could. Beautifying the beach, some would call it. Not me.

I turned to go and as I did I noticed Mattie Morrison on her porch a couple of cottages down on my side of the street. She stood clutching the porch railing, facing the remnants of the Sweeney place. She looked fine but it appeared a few windows on this side of her home were blown out. I was tempted for a second to see if she had anything to say about this or any of the million other things that were gnawing at my brain. But she had what looked like an old crony up on the porch with her and they were chattering away like the elderly do.

I decided to put off that little talk with Mattie. I headed for my car and the High Tide. I had drinks to pour and a head full of questions to ponder.

Chapter 20

EXCEPT FOR TALK of the explosion, work that afternoon was uneventful. As soon as I'd finished my shift around five, I took a walk across Ocean Boulevard and sat on the railing, staring at the ocean, smelling the salty air, and trying to relax a bit. Instead of relaxing, I started to shake. This beach was full of loose cannons and they all seemed to be aimed at me. Problem was—I didn't know which was the one that might fire, which made everything a whole lot worse. There was the visit from Ober Sweeney's girlfriend. She'd made a direct threat and I wasn't sure if it was an idle one. Who knows with crank heads? And for that matter, what about Ober himself? Or Lenny Conklin? Any danger there? And that sleazebag Frankie Earring? And who the hell had almost drowned Shamrock? Cora Sweeney's cottage being vaporized—coincidence? Like hell it was.

If there was any chance that one of these fine citizens did in Cora Sweeney, then I was definitely in danger — the murderer wouldn't be thrilled about my nosing around and getting close to them. The gravity of what I'd gotten myself into percolated through my thick skull and I might have had a full-blown anxiety attack right then and there if I hadn't suddenly become distracted.

A character known as Seagull Sally, one of the locals, was headed directly my way. She was feeding a flock of pigeons and a few seagulls with breadcrumbs she pulled from her windbreaker pocket. The woman was thin as a pipe cleaner and looked like she could use some food, too. The birds trailed along with her as she moved — some walking, others flying circles around her — and when she got within a few yards from me, she stopped and held out her arms like a scarecrow. Some of the birds immediately flew down to roost. One particularly fat grayish-white seagull actually plunked down, like it was laying an egg, right on the duckbilled hat perched on the damn fool's noggin.

She started walking toward me again, birds still perched on her arms and flying along beside her like she was the messiah. I'd seen Seagull Sally a hundred times before but we'd never spoken. This time I almost said something as she passed, deciding against speaking up at the last second. Didn't want her to stop for a chat. Might end up with bird shit all over me. As the mobile bird perch passed by I wondered if Seagull Sally knew that pigeons were filthy birds.

I watched Sally parade down the boardwalk like a feathered tree and made up my mind. The decks were definitely stacked against me—time to even the odds.

I walked back to the cottage, got in my car, drove over the Hampton Bridge, and kept driving till I came to Route 286. I took a few lefts and rights until I came to a long gravel road and turned onto it. A couple of minutes later I passed a large tin sign stuck to a tree that read: Jimbo's Gun Shop & Shooting Range. A little bit further on I pulled up to a small cinderblock building, parked my car, and went in.

On my right were display cases holding various types of firearms. To my left more displays of handguns and ammo. Beyond the displays, the far wall opened up on an indoor firing range. Only a couple of the half-dozen ranges were in use. Retorts of varying volumes sporadically reverberated through the building.

I walked up to the closest display case. There was a very big man standing behind it. He had on jeans, a cowboy hat, and a black T-shirt with the business name stenciled across the chest. I'm not an expert on guns, but he wore a holster on his hip with what looked like some kind of automatic pistol shoved into it. I didn't doubt the pistol was loaded. Considering his size, I wasn't sure what he needed it for.

"Can I help you?" he asked.

I nodded and looked down at the case. This wasn't my first experience with guns—in fact, back at the cottage I kept a sweet little double-barreled 12 gauge under the bed. I'd also had a handgun up until recently. Both guns had come in handy when I'd gotten in that jam with the coke smugglers a while back. But after that little incident was put to bed, I'd hoped my kids would be able to visit me again and decided the handgun was too dangerous to have around. Couldn't bear to part with Betsy though. I kept the shotgun unloaded and the shells hidden. It was good for home defense but it wasn't a walking-around weapon. Judging by the attack on Shamrock and the trouble in the kitchen, it was time to find something a bit handier to have around than Betsy. "I'd like to use a range and rent a pistol."

"No problem. Half-hour or hour?"

"Hour."

"What kind?"

"I'm not sure. Can I use more than one gun in the hour?"

"Use as many as you want. Gotta pay for the ammo though."

"Okay." I was nervous. It had been a long time since I'd even fired a handgun, so I figured I'd best start small. "I'll start with a .22."

I swear I could detect a smirk on the big man's face. He removed a pistol from the display case and placed it in front of me with a light clink. He didn't offer to tell me about the pistol and I didn't care; the .22 wouldn't be my final choice.

He dropped a box of shells beside the gun. "Targets?" He pointed toward a few samples tacked up on the wall.

I chose a black-and-white bull's-eye and he handed me a stack.

I reached for the gun.

"Can't go in there without eye and ear protection."

I'd known that but didn't know the procedure. My mouth felt like the Sahara Desert so I just nodded. He got me a pair of safety glasses and ear protectors that looked like something airplane pilots would wear.

I put the glasses and ear guards on, gathered up the pistol, ammo, and targets and headed across the store in the direction of the range. I barely heard the big man behind me yell, "Use Range Four."

I found number four all right but almost jumped out of my skin when someone fired off what must've been a magnum just a few feet from me. I hooked up one of my targets to the pulley device and sent it down range. My hands shook as I loaded the gun. They shook more as I aimed at my target. I squeezed the trigger slowly and when the retort came it sounded like a baby's fart compared to the shot that had startled me. Still, the first shot from the .22 made me jerk, but after just a few minutes I was firing like I did it all the time.

Before my hour was through I'd also tried a .38 revolver and a .357 magnum. I left Jimbo's with the .38 and several boxes of ammo. I locked it all in my glove box. I didn't realize then that that would be a move I'd soon regret.

Chapter 21

IT WAS DARK when I got out of my car. I'd been think-ing hard on the drive home and had almost reached the first step to my porch when I remembered the revolver in the glove box. Before I could turn back, something hard jammed against the back of my skull. I froze.

"You're not gonna give me a fuckin' problem, are ya?" A man's voice, gravelly and familiar.

"No." There was something ironic about having spent all that time getting a new gun only to find someone else's gun to my head.

"Walk this way and don't look at me and ya got noth-in' to worry about." The gun barrel shoved against my head and I moved forward. We walked around my place, cut between two other cottages, and came out on the next street over. He pushed me toward a black Buick or Olds,

I couldn't tell which, with its back door open. I couldn't see the plate, only the side of the car, but I'd seen this car before. Someone sat in the driver's seat with their head turned away.

"Get in. Lie down and keep your face on the seat." He gave me a shove with his hand between my shoulder blades and I sprawled face down on the back seat. He slid in behind me, pushing my legs out of the way. The gun barrel moved from my head to my ass.

My heart hammered and I fought to control my voice. "What's this all about?" I was pretty sure I already knew the answer.

"Shut up," Gravel Voice said, poking the gun harder against my butt.

I jerked, my face rubbing against the seat's worn material. My nostrils filled with the smell of spilled booze, cigarettes, and dirty dog. My chest tightened as the fumes seeped into my brain, like an accelerant poured on the flames of my anxiety. Right about then I would have given my left nut for a breath of salty Hampton Beach air.

The door slammed and the car started to move. I tried to track our route, forgetting the smells and what my face was plastered to. We took a right when we got up to Ocean Boulevard, an easy guess considering Ocean's a one-way. Being May the traffic was light to non-existent with very few sounds to help identify my location. Then we took a left on what I knew had to be a letter street, then another left on Ashworth, the one-way that runs parallel to Ocean. A few turns later, I was thoroughly confused.

After what might have been ten minutes the car rumbled to a stop. We hadn't driven far enough in any one direction to leave the beach. We had to be either on Ocean, Ashworth, one of the lettered streets, or a back street off Ashworth Avenue.

"I'm gonna put somethin' on your head," Gravel Voice said. "You just go where I tell ya and fast." He tugged some type of hood over my head.

They hustled me out of the car, up three wooden stairs, then we banged through a storm door. The door closed behind us and one of them slammed a wooden door after it. We only took a few steps before I was stopped, my arms pulled roughly behind my back, and my wrists bound tightly with what might've been clothesline rope. Then I was spun around and shoved down on what felt like a sofa. It was like déjà vu. The place reeked of cats, booze, and cigarettes.

Someone yanked the hood off and I had a chance to see what I was up against. I blinked a few times to get my eyes working. They were already tearing from the cat aroma. I was in a rental cottage on the beach. A cheap one, too. The front room looked like the front room of dozens of beach dumps I'd been in through the years, the kind where the landlord rents to anyone, charges top money, lets the joint fall apart, and bleeds the property dry. Kind of like Cora Sweeney's place, only not as clean.

I'd been plunked down on the standard-issue ratty couch. Scattered around the room were the usual suspects—second-hand chairs, banged-up coffee table, and atrocious beach pictures askew on the wall. A small TV over in one corner rested on what looked to be a small tray table. All in all, a pretty depressing room even if you weren't bound with rope and sitting on a sofa about to face who knew what.

And standing directly in front of me were my hosts. There were just the two of them. One short and heavy with a Ronald Reagan mask on his face. In his left hand he held a pistol pointed directly at me. He wore white pants, matching patent leather shoes, a screaming loud Hawaiian shirt opened halfway down his hairy chest, and a thick gold chain around his neck. The attire didn't help identify him; the bandaged right hand did.

Behind him stood a big goon, well over six-two and two hundred pounds. He was dressed normally except for the rubber clown mask with a big red nose covering his face and a "Born to Die" tattoo on his forearm. I wondered for a moment what his puss looked like under that mask, then realized I was probably better off not knowing.

The two jokers stood there staring down at me, not moving except for the occasional blink. They didn't say anything, but they didn't have to. They were making me plenty nervous. I felt the anxiety seeping through me and I couldn't tell what was natural for the situation

I was in and what was the beginning of something else. I took a deep breath and let it out slow. It didn't help. I thought about the prescription bottle in my pocket— maybe I could fake heart problems and get these jerks to slip me a pill. Then again, heart problems might be exactly what they'd want.

It didn't look like they were in any hurry to talk, so I swallowed hard and said, "What the hell's this all about?"

"It's trick or treat," said the big goon, sounding like a kid getting ready for Halloween. I could almost see the sneer behind his mask. "What's with the sha...a...a...ky voice? You a scaredy-cat or something?"

The short guy, the one with the gravelly voice, half turned to his partner. "Shut ya pie hole. This isn't any joke. It's business." Then he looked back at me. "What it is, ass-hole, is how many times you gotta be told—butt outta what don't concern ya? You gotta learn to keep your trap shut once and for all. Capisce?"

My anxiety was bad and getting worse and even if it hadn't been, this was no time to play hero. "I think I've learned."

Gravel Voice shook his head. "Na, na, na. Nice try, but you don't get out of it that easy. Your lesson hasn't even started yet. Besides you owe me plenty." He held up his bandaged right hand and shook it. "That didn't tickle and I'm gonna have a scar too."

"Sorry about that," I said stupidly.

"My turn now?" the goon asked. He kept balling and unballing his huge fists. "Can I? Huh?"

"Hold your freakin' horses, dimwit," Gravel Voice commanded. "I think we're gonna help Marlowe here heighten the experience just a little bit." He let out the kind of laugh you'd probably hear in an insane asylum.

My voice shook again. "Look, I won't be asking any more questions, all right? I'm out of it." And at that moment I meant it.

"I already know that, asshole," Gravel Voice said. "Now open your mouth."

I wasn't sure what he was up to but I was positive no one was gonna open my mouth, not even if they had a crowbar. Boy, was I wrong. Gravel Voice made a disgusted sound, then said, "Bozo, open his mouth."

The big man pulled what looked like a .357 magnum revolver from his waistband. He walked over to me and touched the barrel against my lips. "Open the fuck up," he said.

My mouth opened as wide as the Hampton Bridge. The gun slid in as easy as if it was going into a twenty dollar whore. And in that moment I would've given up my mother for a couple of those pills in my jeans pocket.

I couldn't see anything except the mile-long barrel running from my open mouth. I swallowed hard, trying not to gag on the oily taste. I shuddered at the thought of the damage the deadly cold barrel could do to my fear-riddled brain. I was beyond being scared.

Somewhere in the background Gravel Voice started asking questions. "Now we aren't going to have any more problems with you, are we, shithead? No more questions on the beach or anywhere else. Right?"

I nodded up and down, my teeth bumping against the sea-blue gun metal.

"Let's find out if he means it, Bozo."

The big guy grunted. The world focused on one single point—the pistol's hammer as it moved slowly away from my face. My anus puckered and I struggled to control my bladder. Time stretched for an eternity, then—bang! The hammer slammed down hard, steel against steel. The barrel jerked against my teeth, but the nuclear explosion I'd been expecting turned into a loud dud. I gagged and almost spewed whatever I'd had in my stomach all over that friggin' gun barrel. At the same time I started hyperventilating and would have given both nuts for a bag to breathe into. Reagan and Bozo laughed as if they'd just shared their first joint.

"We was only foolin' ya," Bozo said as he worked the hammer quickly five more times. The dry firing didn't bother me; I was too far gone.

Gravel Voice choked back his laughter and said, "You shoulda seen your face. I don't think we'll have to worry about you again, will we?"

I shook my head, again banging my teeth against the cold metal, but I didn't care.

I was going to live! Get another chance to make things right with my kids and Sharon. The relief swept over me like a tsunami. Good thing I wasn't standing—my legs felt so weak I probably would have collapsed.

I was so busy thinking about all the living I had left to do, I didn't pay attention to Bozo until I realized he was balling and unballing his other fist again. "Now, Ronnie, now?"

"How about tellin' us where the kid is, Marlowe?"

I shook my head slowly, mindful of the barrel still in my mouth.

"All right," Gravel Voice said. "If that's the way you want to play it." He took the gun from Bozo's hand and removed it from my mouth, slowly dragging the metal across my teeth.

"See if you can find out where the kid is," Gravel Voice said to Bozo. "Just don't get fuckin' carried away. I know how much you like this part, but we ain't gettin' paid to kill anyone. Just a nice easy beating. Can you do that?"

"Sure I can. Whattaya think I am, an amatoor?"

"All right, then. I ain't watching. I gotta weak stomach. I'll be out front havin' a smoke. Call me when you're through. And remember, don't get carried away. And Marlowe, I hope you learned your lesson. Keep your nose outta other people's business or we'll do this dance again. And next time it'll be your last dance." He turned and left the cottage.

"Just you and me now, Pally," Bozo said. Then he balled both huge fists, held them up like a boxer, and spit first on one, then the other. Suddenly, all the fear and anxiety built up inside exploded and I thrashed around on the sofa, struggling to break my bonds. No way I was going to sit still and take a beating now that there wasn't a gun put to my head.

The first blows sent me where the fear hadn't let me go — deep enough into oblivion that I didn't feel the rest.

Chapter 22

ONE EYE POPPED OPEN; the other eye felt like it was glued shut. I stared up at the unfamiliar ceiling and wondered how I'd ended up flat on my back. I ran my tongue around the inside of my mouth, grimacing at the taste of blood and vomit. Pain came in drum-like beats, mostly from my face. I raised my hand and tentatively did a little exploring. My face was still there—a little rearranged maybe, but basically in one piece. My nostrils were stuffed up, but they still worked—I could smell cats, booze, and butts again.

I sat up on the sofa, put my feet on the floor, stood up. Took three steps before I stumbled and grabbed the wall for support. I hung on there for a minute, waiting for the world to stop spinning around. Finally I took a deep breath and headed for the door. I made it to the door, took another breath, and went out into the bright moonlight. The light jabbed my one good eye like a rusty knife. I grabbed my head and struggled to stay on my feet.

After a while the pain subsided to the point where I could see again. I was on the porch of a cottage on J Street... or K Street...maybe L Street...some goddamn lettered street. I could hear an occasional car up on Ocean and could make out the shadows of buildings around me. I was hurt bad and I knew it. I'd never make it to my cottage and I couldn't stand here—wherever the hell I was. I needed to get cleaned up, fixed up. No use turning to the cops—I'd been warned. There was just one place I could come up with, a place I might be able to make it to.

I stumbled down the stairs and lurched down the street like a drunken bum who'd just been mugged. I made it to Ashworth, followed the road for about fifty yards, and then limped like the Hunchback across the street. One car zigzagged around me, the driver yelling something that didn't register.

I continued along Ashworth for a short distance. When I reached the street I was looking for, I turned down it. A few kids standing in front of Cora Sweeney's empty lot drinking beer saw me coming and scattered. I limped to the one place I might find help—Mattie Morrison's cottage. I took the few steps to the porch, pulled myself up by the railing, and knocked on the front door. If it didn't open, I didn't know what I'd do. I knocked again.

Inside a light went on. The door slowly swung open and there she was—Mattie Morrison—in a robe and one of those hairnets like my mother used to wear.

"Dan Marlowe. Sweet mother of mercy." She reached out and grabbed my arm just as my legs collapsed. My arm draped around her shoulder and she actually supported me as I stumbled into her front room. She was the strongest little old woman I'd ever seen. She was a regular Granny Clampett in strength, heart, and looks.

With her help I lowered myself down onto an easy chair, Mattie snatching her knitting up before I sat on it. I slowly put my throbbing head on the back of the chair. Mattie looked down at me and gently took my face in her icy hands. The cold calmed the fire burning in my face.

"Good Lawd. Ya don't look good, Dan. That eye's bad. Ya gotta get to the hospital."

"No, Mattie," I croaked. "I can't. No hospitals." I was in enough hot water without the police and newspapers finding out.

She studied me as if debating whether or not to ignore my request.

"All right. I'll do the best I can. But if ya take a turn for the worse, you're goin' whether ya like it or not. Fair?"

I nodded and winced.

Mattie hurried out of the room. I looked around, trying to focus on something beside the pain. It was a clean cottage; that didn't surprise me. But everything in it — furniture, pictures, curtains — was from another time. She took pride in her little space, though. Nothing was out of place. The house didn't smell bad, just the smell you sometimes notice in a very old person's home. The last time I'd smelled that smell was in my grandmother's house when I was a boy.

Mattie came bustling back into the room moving faster than I thought anyone that age could. I watched her with my one good eye. She carried a huge silver serving tray. She placed the tray on an old, maybe even antique, coffee table a couple of feet from me in front of a flowered love seat. On the tray sat a box of assorted bandages, antiseptic, washcloth, glass of water, cotton balls, and a few things I didn't recognize. There was also a medium-sized bowl filled almost to the top with steaming water.

"How much are ya hurtin', Dan?" she asked.

I didn't answer.

"That's what I thought." She took some pills from the tray and handed them to me. "Try these. They're for my arthritis. Perco...something. I take one but you better take a couple more."

She'd handed me three; I washed them down with the glass of water she held to my lips.

"I'm gonna clean ya up. It's probably gonna hurt some."

She dipped the cloth in the hot water and touched my face gently. I grimaced and gritted my teeth. Mattie kept up a constant stream of conversation while she worked.

"It was Ober Sweeney done this, wasn't it?" She nodded rapidly. "I knew there'd be trouble from that low-life. He's a no-good."

I mumbled words when she wasn't tending to my mouth. "I don't know, Mattie. I couldn't tell who the hell it was. Masks. Reagan and a clown."

"Ha! Comedians too. Bums coulda killed ya."

She continued to work on my face. I looked at her hands. She wore a wedding ring with a tiny diamond. There was a fold of flesh surrounding the ring. How many decades had the ring been on that finger? I wondered. When had the ring been last off and could it even be removed? Her nails looked manicured. Her slate grey eyes looked like the ocean after a storm. The lines on her face were as deep as canyons yet somehow her skin was as smooth as a baby's butt. Her hands stopped.

"Dan?"

I heard her. I wanted to answer; I couldn't. The pills had done their blessed work.

Chapter 23

I DON'T KNOW HOW LONG I was out but when I woke up, the first thing I saw was Steve Moore looking at me. He was perched on a straight back chair directly in front of me, wearing his customary short-sleeved shirt and tie. He gave me a minute to come around, then pursed his lips, and shook his head. "I told you to stop poking around, Dan. Now look what's happened."

I still felt plenty bad; it'd take more than a little nap to change that. But in spite of a sore mouth and an iron taste I could still talk. "Yeah, you did, didn't you." I glanced around the room.

"Mrs. Morrison's not here. She was plenty upset and besides I wanted to talk to you myself. I walked her over to her friend's a couple doors down."

"She didn't waste any time calling you."

Steve smiled. "It wasn't her. Some kids called about a drunken bloody maniac down on Reed Street. I guess you sobered them up fast. I was on duty. Didn't have much trouble figuring out where the maniac had gone. And I wasn't too surprised to find out the maniac in question was you. When I got here you were out and she'd fixed you up like Florence Nightingale." He put his hands on his knees and leaned closer. "You still don't look great. Hospital?"

I shook my head, then wished I hadn't. "No, I'll be all right."

Steve flipped his hands up. "Well, I'd still get checked by a doc. 'Specially that eye."

I didn't like how everyone kept mentioning my eye; that couldn't be good. My heart sped up. "Okay. How long have I been asleep?"

"Few hours." Steve crossed his legs at the ankles and folded his arms across his chest. "So let's get down to business. What the hell happened?"

My mind was still foggy, like the beach at sunrise. The Percs were not only working on the pain but on my mind too. Yeah, Steve thought I was a little flaky, but this might be my last chance to convince him that Cora Sweeney's death was more than an accident. After all, I couldn't have beaten myself. "Someone doesn't want me asking questions about Cora Sweeney."

"Even I have that motive."

I pointed to my face. "Yeah, but you wouldn't do this to me."

Steve laughed. "Look, I told you to stay out of this. The broad's death was an accident, nothing more. You're just stirring up trouble. Trouble that bounced back on you. You got the shit kicked outta you, and excuse me for saying it, but you probably deserved it. People got other things on the beach they want to hide and they don't want a clown like you bumbling across it. Probably had nothing to do with Cora Sweeney."

He was a tough nut and not easy to convince, but I wanted to see how tough he really was. "The guys that worked me over wanted to know how to find Kelsey Sweeney."

Steve looked alarmed for an instant, then wiped all expression off his face. "They asked you that?"

"Yep."

"What'd you tell them?"

"Nothing. I don't know where Kelsey is and I wouldn't have told them if I did."

"They say what they wanted him for?"

"No. But it's pretty obvious, isn't it? Someone thinks Kelsey saw whoever killed his mother."

Steve looked pissed. "Then they think wrong. No one killed his mother."

I saw an opening and took it. "Why do they want him then? I tell you, Steve, Kelsey's in danger."

Steve stood up. Pushed his chair back with his foot. "Okay, maybe he is. But we still haven't had any luck finding him even though he's been spotted a couple times on the beach. Fast little sucker on that skateboard.

Besides, a runaway kid isn't a priority. Has he come to see you again?"

I shook my head and groaned. Even with the Percs my head felt like it'd been stomped by a Hampton Police horse.

"Well, if he does come to see you again, you better hold onto him for us. *If* you're as concerned as you say you are."

"Believe me, someone wants Kelsey bad. Maybe finding him should be a priority."

"That's probably a good idea."

I blinked. Had Steve actually agreed with me?

Steve waved at my face. I winced. "Now what about this? Any idea who did it?" He took the small notebook and pen from his shirt pocket, flicked the pen.

"Ronald Reagan and Bozo the Clown."

"Very funny. Cut the comedy and give me something I can use."

"It was the same character who pistol-whipped the cook at the Tide. His hand was bandaged."

"You're lucky he didn't light your hair on fire. What else?"

"That's about it. They wore masks. Grabbed me at the cottage, had me eating carpet lint for a roundabout ride. I could tell I ended up at some rundown cottage on one of the lettered streets."

"How do you know that?

"I've been hanging around Hampton Beach my whole life. It's just not that big. The lettered streets aren't taken from the Chinese alphabet."

Steve chuckled. "Can you narrow it down any?"

"L, K...J or I maybe." I could remember little of my walk to Mattie's house.

"Would you recognize it if you saw it again."

"From the inside."

"Can you describe the cottage at all?"

I shook my head, remembering to do it slowly. "Not the outside. I was in a fog when I came out of there. The inside was a dump. So that probably means it was a rental. A live-in owner'd never let it go like that. "

"That sure doesn't narrow it down much. How many guys were there?"

"Just the two."

"Description?"

"I couldn't see much. Like I said, they wore masks."

He didn't say anything, just kept looking at me. I wondered if he had a good memory; he wasn't writing any of this down after all. Then I realized there wasn't that much to remember.

Steve flicked the pen and returned pen and notebook to his shirt pocket. "All right. I'll look into it."

"What about Kelsey?"

"I'll get a stepped-up search for him going. I don't know why these shitheads want him, but I don't want them catching up to him before we do." He reached down and grabbed my arm.

"Come on. I'll give you a ride home. Although I really should be giving you a ride to Exeter Hospital."

"I'm all right," I lied.

Steve helped me to my feet. My legs wobbled. The drugs were beginning to wear off and my face felt like I'd gone a few rounds with Mike Tyson. Still, it was nothing compared to the anxiety building in my psyche that would soon, I knew, have physical effects. I could have taken a pill, but not in front of Steve.

Steve had barely left after driving me home when a sense of dread suddenly flooded over me. My heart started jackhammering and my mouth dried up like beach sand. I took two steps, hoping to make it to the kitchen and a beer but the floor tilted like a funhouse walkway. I scrambled in my jeans pocket and dragged out the prescription bottle with shaking hands. I fumbled off the cap, spilling several pills to the floor. I didn't care; I'd get them later. I plopped two pills under my tongue, careened to the refrigerator, and grabbed an entire six-pack.

Then I made it to my chair and held on, waiting for the storm to pass.

Chapter 24

I'M A LIGHT SLEEPER. Even in the condition I was in, the knocking at the door woke me. When I opened my eye I saw that it was dark out. It took a minute before I realized I'd been out cold all day. I was still sitting in the chair I'd plopped into after taking the pills. The knocking persisted. I thought of grabbing Betsy from under my bed but suddenly the bedroom seemed an eternity away.

I cleared my throat. "Who is it?" My voice sounded strange, like someone else's.

"Dan, it's me. Dianne. Let me in, please."

I knew instantly what she wanted—I'd missed my shift at work. I hadn't even called her, an oversight I'd never made before, even on my worst days. I glanced at the phone beside me and vaguely remembered turning off the ringer. My shirt was stained with blood. The rest of me probably looked like I'd been in a barroom brawl. I didn't want to scare Dianne but there was nothing I could do about it now.

"Dan, are you all right?"

"I'm coming." I pulled myself up from my chair, feeling like a ship that'd just cracked up on the jetty. Between being beaten to a pulp, doped up on pills and beer, worrying about everything that'd gone wrong in my life, and facing Dianne, I was a mess. I flipped on a lamp, dragged myself the few steps to the front door, and opened it.

Dianne stood just inside the storm door. She was a good actress, but she wasn't that good. She made a decent attempt to hide the shock on her face, but couldn't hide it at all from her voice.

"Oh, my god. What happened?" She grabbed my arm and baby-stepped me back to my chair. She helped me sit back down, then stood over me liked a worried hen. I hadn't seen her away from work in I didn't know how long. No restaurant whites today—jeans, an expensive-looking black leather jacket, and a red silk blouse wrapped around a body that didn't eat much fattening restaurant food. Her black hair hung loose around her shoulders and a light dusting of makeup touched her eyes and cheeks. Looked like I'd interrupted Dianne's evening plans. Her green eyes glittered in the dim lamplight.

"I had a little bit of trouble," I said.

She backed up to the sofa and sat on the edge without taking her eyes off my face. "A little bit of trouble? Are you all right? Have you been to the hospital?" Her voice cracked.

"I'm okay. I look a lot worse than I am."

"I hope so." She wasn't joking; she looked plenty concerned. She shifted into Boss mode. "Dan, I want to know what the hell is going on. You avoided most of the questions I asked you after Guillermo got hurt. Now Shamrock's in the hospital, you get beaten up, that Mrs. Sweeney's place blows up. I want to know right now, Dan Marlowe. Tell me what's going on before...before someone's killed." She leaned forward and gave me what she probably thought was a threatening stare.

Dianne couldn't scare me. Not after what I'd been through. What did scare me was the thought of anything happening to her because of what I was involved in. She had a right to know—not only was her business being impacted but she needed to take measures to protect herself. Just in case.

She raised her voice, "Dan?"

I told her the whole story. Everything I knew and even my guesses. She fidgeted a few times but otherwise just sat and listened. I didn't realize I'd made the wrong decision to tell her until she spoke. Then it was too late to take it all back.

She jumped up. "We're going to the police right now. Come on."

"Dianne, I already told them everything," I said softly, trying to calm her down.

She threw her hands up in frustration. "What'd they say?"

"They're looking into it."

Dianne's voice went up an octave. "Looking into it? Someone could die while they're looking into it."

Looked like I'd really screwed up telling her the whole story. I should have given her a censored version. Now I had to stop her from doing something that would make things even worse. "Steve Moore's checking into it. He's good. You know that."

"Maybe, but you told me he doesn't believe any of what you've told me. This is bullshit, Dan. I'm not going to stand by and do nothing while someone might hurt you again or worse." She hesitated, then added quickly. "Or Shamrock or Guillermo."

Dianne never swore, so I knew I was in trouble.

"If the police can't help us," she continued, "we'll get someone else. Between us we know a lot of people."

Now it was "us." I didn't like that. No use dropping her in the mix with me and Shamrock. I had to stop it now.

"Dianne, I've got an idea," I lied. If I could keep her busy for a while maybe I could come up with a plan.

"I've got an idea too. What about Tiny?"

Good god, Tiny. The man would give you the shirt off his back if he liked you. A very big shirt. And he liked us both. But if Tiny got involved, all bets were off. He'd go around the beach like a damn bull in a china shop. He'd done it before.

I had to short circuit this quick. "Let me try my idea, Dianne. It's a good one. If you tell Tiny or anybody else what's going on, you could throw it off track. If my little plan works, no one's going to get hurt and everything will be over. You've got to give me some time."

She sat back on the edge of the sofa and gave me a skeptical look. "How long?"

I threw out numbers I hoped were reasonable. "Four or five days." I'd never been much of a liar but since this little "adventure" had started I'd done more lying than a used car salesman. I'd make it up to everyone later. Right now all that mattered was protecting the people I cared for.

She looked at me for a long time. "All right, Dan. I hope you know what you're doing."

"I do." If I kept this up, my nose was going to be longer than Ocean Boulevard.

"Okay, I guess." Dianne stood up and gave me another long look, and for a second I saw something there that I'd never noticed before, all mixed in with the worry and fear. She turned toward the door, then hesitated. Before I could ask what was wrong, she came over to my easy chair and sat on the arm. She seemed nervous; unusual for her. Her face reddened just a bit and there was that look in her eyes again.

She wrapped her arm gently around my head and pulled my banged-up face to her chest. I felt the red silk and her breasts through it. She gave off a wonderful scent.

She held me like that for I don't know how long. The hug felt good but I didn't know what it meant. Probably just taking pity on me. After all, I'd known for a long time I was a pretty pitiful character.

Eventually, she sat up and held my face gently with both hands. She looked into my eyes. "Are you going to be all right here tonight? Do you want company?"

Of course I did, but I couldn't. And besides, the longer she hung around me the more chance someone would think she was involved somehow. "I'll be all right. Honest."

"You'd better be, Dan Marlowe. I need you...at the restaurant." She turned for the door. "Don't think of coming in 'til you're feeling better. I don't want you scaring the customers."

Funny. I watched her leave, closing the door behind her.

Chapter 25

FRIDAY, the beginning of the big Memorial Day weekend, and I hadn't left my cottage since Steve Moore had dropped me off. I'd slept again after Dianne had left the night before, but I still felt like shit, both physically and mentally. I didn't have to go to work; Dianne had made that clear. I couldn't have gotten through a shift anyhow. Maybe I'd feel human enough by Monday or Tuesday to make it back to work.

I checked out my face in the mirror. Good thing I hadn't eaten anything—I would've lost it right then and there. It'd been a long time since I'd had a black eye, especially one swollen shut tight as a clam. Various bruises and cuts decorated the rest of my face; none too deep, luckily. I felt a little better as the day wore on. By late afternoon I was actually attempting to run a razor blade around my battered face, skillfully avoiding the tender areas. I'd been on a liquid diet all day and I was hungry enough to eat a lifeguard's chair.

Around six I decided to step out on my porch and walk down the few steps to the sand. It was still light out, crisp but not cold. The air smelled and felt great. I fired up the gas grill. Traffic rumbled by up on Ocean Boulevard, people coming in to fill up the hotels and motels for the holiday weekend. I'd always loved Memorial Day weekend, knowing summer had finally arrived and the whole wonderful beach season stretched out in front of me. I adjusted the grill knobs, wondering if maybe I'd actually feel like taking a walk uptown later that evening. I chuckled to myself — the fact I could even think about a walk like that was a good sign.

I stepped back up on the porch, waiting for the grill to heat up, and that's when I heard the unmistakable clickety-clack of a skateboard coming down the street. Visions of my son sprang into my head. But instead, Kelsey Sweeney rolled around the corner of the cottage in front of mine, then barreled down the walkway right up to the porch steps and hopped off his board. He stepped on the skateboard tail, popped the board up, snatched it out of the air, and stuck it under his arm.

I stood on the porch looking down at him. He stood there looking up at me like he was waiting for an invitation. So I gave him a quick nod. Kelsey set the board down and bounded up the stairs. For a moment I thought he was going to hug me—I wouldn't have minded—but he just stood there looking uncomfortable. It had been more than a week since his mother had died. He'd been alone on the beach all that time and he looked it. He had on the same clothes as the last time I'd seen him with an added week's worth of dirt caked on.

"How did you know where I lived?" I finally asked.

"I followed you from the restaurant one time."

I wanted to ask him some other questions, important questions, but I didn't want to scare him away. So instead I said, "Can you eat some hot dogs?"

I might as well've asked him if he'd like to turn skateboard pro. He nodded so hard my head hurt just watching him.

"How many can you eat?" I watched him start to calculate. "Never mind. I got an unopened package in the fridge that's still good. I'll throw 'em all on. Save me two though, will you?" He nodded again.

"While I'm doing that why don't you take a quick shower. You got half the sand on Hampton Beach on you. I got some clean clothes you can wear."

He didn't seem as happy about the shower as he did about the hot dogs but he didn't give me any argument. In fact, I got the impression he was glad someone was telling him what to do. I walked him through the cottage and showed him where the bathroom was. The bathroom wasn't big—just enough room for a sink, toilet, and shower—but he didn't need big to get clean. I got him a towel and facecloth and left him alone. Then I went into the bedroom closest to the bathroom — my son's old room. Like most beach cottage bedrooms the room was small with only a bed, bureau, and large oval mirror on the wall. Baseball caps, remnants of my son's collection, hung on wooden pegs along the wall beside the mirror.

I went to the bureau and rummaged through the drawers. There wasn't too much his mother had left behind, but I was lucky. I came across a skateboard T-shirt with a colorful Powell & Peralta logo emblazoned on it, along with a pair of baggy jeans shorts that the circus fat lady could have fit into. That's the way kids liked them though. I also found a pair of underpants and some socks, and set the whole bunch of stuff, along with one of my pocket combs and a belt, just inside the bathroom door. I could hear the water running hard in the shower.

While Kelsey worked on getting rid of a week's worth of dirt, I worked on supper. Fifteen minutes later he opened the bathroom door and stepped into the kitchen, looking like a new boy. He seemed pleased with what I'd picked out for him to wear. He stared down at the design on his chest, cocking his head and trying to read it upside down. Then he looked back toward the bathroom. "What should I do with my dirty clothes?"

"Don't worry about that. I'll wash them for you. Here. Sit down." I nodded toward a chair at the kitchen table. I had the table all set up with a pile of dogs on a large platter, hot dog rolls, two bowls of steaming baked beans, chips, pickles, and all the fixings. By the way his eyes snapped open, I could tell he approved of the spread too.

I'd never seen anyone, except myself, slather so much yellow mustard on a hot dog. When the two of us came up for air, six of the puppies had disappeared, along with the beans and the better part of a gallon of milk.

"I guess you were hungry, huh?"

He nodded and gave me a smile wide enough to almost split his face. The smile quickly disappeared as he pointed a long bony finger at my face. "What happened?"

"I fell off the jetty."

His voice quivered. "Did it hurt?"

"No. It's better now. Just looks bad."

He looked at me doubtfully, seemed about to say something more, and then yawned. A real yawn, the kind kids can't control. No shower was going to wash the smudge under his eyes away, only sleep would do that. "Kelsey, I think you better sleep here tonight. In my son's room. He's not here right now."

Kelsey didn't answer, but I could tell he wanted to stay. Sleeping under cottages would grow old, even for a kid, after a while. "Would you rather go to your father's house?" I asked, shamelessly feeling him out.

He looked frightened, flicked his hair back off his face, and shook his head. Good thing. I wouldn't have taken him anyway.

I led him to my son's bedroom and pulled back the covers on the bed. He started to lie down. "I don't think there's any pajamas here but you can sleep in your underwear if you want. Hang your clothes on the hook on the back of the door. We'll talk in the morning. I'll be right out front."

He didn't move and for a second he could have been my son laying there. "Okay," was all he said.

I left the bedroom, closed the door behind me, and headed back out to the porch. Night had fallen and the sky was splashed with stars. It was a little cool, but I didn't care. By the traffic sounds off in the distance the strip was busier than it had been for months. I couldn't do my walk now, not at night anyway, not with Kelsey here. The same guys who'd almost beaten me into oblivion were after the boy. I wasn't going to let them get their hands on him.

I sat on the porch, rocking like an old man, for a long time and didn't have a single Heineken. I thought and got myself nowhere, just hoping that eventually I'd be able to sleep. And when I thought maybe I could, I got up. Just before I went back inside, I caught a glimpse of something on the walkway at the bottom of the porch steps. I went down, picked up Kelsey's skateboard, took it in the cottage, and hid it under my bed beside Betsy. And I realized just how tired a boy he must've been to forget that skateboard. After all, it was all he had left, wasn't it?

Chapter 26

THE NEXT MORNING I woke up early after a lousy night's sleep and decided to attempt a run on the beach. A couple of my ribs were still sore and a deep breath was painful, but jogging is addictive and my guilt wouldn't let me skip it any longer. I debated leaving the boy alone, but no one knew he was here, it was daylight, and I wouldn't be long. I locked the door behind me and made it all the way to the jetty and back, only about a quarter of what I usually ran. But it was a start.

Though the run itself was pretty pathetic, more like a walk, I had time to think about what I was going to do about Kelsey. Whoever had worked me over was serious—they could have easily killed me. Just thinking those same guys were looking for Kelsey got my stomach all in knots. There were quite a few names I could come

up with at this point as likely suspects in all this may-
hem. How long would it take for one of these characters to find a young boy on Hampton Beach? He'd been
lucky so far, living under cottages and eating who knew
what, but whoever was looking for him only had to be
lucky once and that would be it.

I couldn't tell Steve Moore that Kelsey had shown up.
I trusted Steve and would help him where I could, but he
was the type who went by the book. He might be forced
by higher ups to turn the boy over to his father, a low-
life and possibly a murderer, if Cora Sweeney had really
been murdered. Not to mention that Kelsey would also
come in contact with his father's girlfriend, Mona Freeman, an even more likely murder suspect. I couldn't let
Kelsey fall into the grasp of either of those people.

Kelsey wasn't up when I returned to the cottage. Not
surprising since he probably hadn't had a good night's
sleep since he'd started crashing on the sand under
cottages.

Around noon I heard the bedroom door creak open
and he came out. His long blonde hair was mussed up
but the circles under his eyes were gone. The sleep and
the food he'd had the night before had made him look
like a normal, healthy kid again.

"You hungry?" I asked. He nodded.

I can't cook much of anything besides hot dogs, but
I had him sit at the kitchen table while I threw some
things together. I filled a huge bowl with Raisin Bran,

sliced a banana on top of the cereal, and then dumped in some milk. I set the bowl in front of him along with a big glass of orange juice and a buttered blueberry muffin. I grabbed a muffin and a glass of milk for myself and sat at the table across from him.

"How did you sleep, Kelsey?"

He'd just shoveled some cereal into his mouth and a little milk dribbled down his chin as he answered. "Okay."

"You left your skateboard outside last night."

He looked up, cereal forgotten.

"Don't worry. I brought it in."

"Thanks," he said with a grin, then went back to demolishing his cereal. The muffin disappeared in three bites.

Sooner or later I had to ask him some questions that I wasn't looking forward to. Looked like now was as bad a time as any other. "Kelsey, last night you said you didn't want to go to your father's. Why?"

He held a heaping spoonful of cereal in mid-air, didn't look at me. "I dunno."

"You don't like him?"

The boy's voice cracked when he answered. "He doesn't like me."

I could believe that; Ober Sweeney probably didn't like anyone. I decided to cut to the chase. "Did he ever hit you?" Kelsey turned red. Christ, looked like he'd been knocked around by half the creeps on the beach.

"Was it your father you heard talking to your mother the night she died?"

It would have made life so easy if he'd said yes.

"I couldn't tell who it was and I didn't care then. I didn't know they were going to hurt Ma." He struggled to hold the tears back. "I would've helped her. She was my mother."

I reached over and touched his arm. "It wasn't your fault. You're right. You didn't know what was going to happen."

He didn't break down though I thought he might. Instead he looked me right in the eye. "Mr. Marlowe..."

"You can call me Dan."

"Dan, have you found out who killed my mother yet?"

"No, not yet. But I will, I promise." I wasn't really sure how I'd fulfill that promise, but there was no way I wasn't going to give it everything I could. "Tell me about this Frankie Earring that owns the T-shirt shop. Were you stealing stuff for him?"

He sat up straight. "Only once, Mr...ahh, Dan. Honest." His face flushed. "The big kids told me about him and I sold him a couple little things I took from a cottage, but no one was living there. Ma found out and almost killed me. She called him up and yelled at him. I don't know what she said. I never went by his store again. I used to skate on the other side of the street so I wouldn't have to go by his store."

"What about a guy named Ted Norris, a real estate agent? You know him?

He shook his head and chewed on his food at the same time. Then he stopped and said, "Hey, maybe he was the man who tried to catch me the other day."

"What man?"

He waved his hands in the air. "Some man chased me through three streets. I finally hid on a porch and he couldn't find me."

"Maybe it was someone who didn't want you sleeping under his cottage."

He shook his head, blonde hair swinging. "No, he kept yelling my name while he was chasing me."

"It might have been a Hampton police detective."

Kelsey looked embarrassed and said, "Nope." I realized that a street kid like him probably knew all the plainclothes cops on the beach.

"What did he look like?"

"He was real big. I was scared."

"Did you notice anything else?"

Kelsey thought for a moment. "I peeked over the porch when he went by. He had a tattoo right here." He pointed to his right forearm.

"A tattoo? Of what?"

He shook his head. "Something about dying."

Bingo. My big friend, Bozo. It had to be. Dirty bastard. If he'd been chasing the boy, it meant I'd been right— Kelsey was in real danger. I looked at the thin blonde boy sitting in front of me and shuddered. If that Neanderthal had gotten hold of him...I suddenly felt guilty that I hadn't worked harder to find Kelsey. Then again—if the whole Hampton police force couldn't find him, I wouldn't have had any luck either. I'd gone in the right direction—after the killer.

"That settles it. You're staying here for a while." I grabbed my coffee cup and took it over to the sink.

Kelsey grinned in relief. "You mean it, Dan? I can stay here with you?"

"Of course, I mean it. At least until we find out what the hell's going on."

He sat up straight in his chair. "We will, Dan. I know we will." Then he suddenly slumped. "Where is my mother?"

I didn't know how to answer. I remembered that Steve Moore said she might have been already buried, but I didn't know where.

"Is she with Nana and Gramp? She always said she wanted to be in the cemetery with them."

I had no idea but I answered, "Yes, Kelsey, I think that's where she is."

I wanted to get his mind off the subject and there was one more thing I needed to point out anyway. I picked up his bowl and glass, set them in the sink, then waved at him to follow me. I led him into the middle bedroom, the one my daughter used to use. I pointed up to a small square trapdoor in the tiny closet. "Can you get yourself up there quickly if you have to?"

He stepped around me, put his foot on a clothes hamper, and boosted himself up, pushing the trapdoor out of his way. He disappeared quickly up into the dark little attic. Then his smiling face filled the hole, looking at me upside down. "Easy," he said.

I smiled back. "Good. If you're ever here alone and someone comes to the door, I want you to get up there as quick as you can, shut the trapdoor, and don't come out until I come back. And be quiet. Okay?"

"Okay, Dan. So we're going to find out who hurt my mother?"

"Yes, Kelsey, we are." And I meant it.

Chapter 27

KELSEY SPENT THE REST of the weekend with me. We watched the fireworks on Sunday night, a Hampton Beach Memorial Day tradition, from my porch. That was as close as I dared to let the boy get to other people. Someone had hired the goons who attacked me and I didn't know who that someone might be.

I didn't get any further looking into who killed his mother. It wasn't just the beating—I really didn't know what the hell to do. I was kind of hoping if I let my subconscious mind work on the problem, it would come up with a solution, but so far all I'd done was recuperate.

I gave Dianne a call and told her I'd be in the next day. She said she'd be there to see me when I came in. So Monday morning I made Kelsey promise he wouldn't leave the cottage, he'd keep the door locked, wouldn't answer any knock, and reminded him about the trapdoor in the closet ceiling. Then I left him alone and headed for the High Tide.

Ocean Boulevard was as crowded as it should be on a holiday. The weatherman had forecast good weather, and by the looks of the bright blue sky and warm temperature he was going to be right for a change. Ahead, I could see the municipal parking lot already filling up. I crossed to the other side of Ocean and headed north. The screams of sirens pierced the air, a natural part of the beach sounds during the summer season. Sometimes there were so many sirens you'd think the nuclear power plant was on fire; usually it was nothing more than tempers flaring in the hot weather.

The smell that suddenly hit my nose wasn't normal though, summer season or not. Something was burning. Something big. I broke into a run. As soon as I passed a miniature golf course with a forty-foot-tall pirate I saw the source of the smell. A few blocks ahead I could see black smoke billowing into the sky and the flashing lights of fire engines and police cars. People from all directions converged on the scene. The sidewalk was jammed with pedestrians headed in that direction. I stepped out into the street to try and get around them. I didn't like the direction the smoke was coming from. I didn't like it at all. My stomach churned.

The closer I got, the sicker I felt. I shoved my way through another knot of people and froze, staring at the smoke curling over the High Tide. I hustled across Ocean Boulevard and hurried up the parking lot side until I was directly across from the restaurant. There were at least five fire engines, two from neighboring Seabrook. Hoses stretched across the street like slithering snakes. A Hampton cop diverted boulevard traffic down a side street a block before the fire. Firemen scurried in and out of the restaurant's front door.

The damage didn't seem as bad up close as I'd feared from a distance. Yes, there was smoke. It seemed to be coming from the kitchen area, out the back of the building, curling over the roof and rising into the blue sky. But I couldn't see any flames. Besides, if the firefighters were going into the building, they must have a handle on it.

The throng of people around me pointed and talked amongst themselves. Beside me stood a short older man, thin gray hair and large eyeglasses. I recognized him as a beach local. "What happened?" I asked.

"Some type of explosion, I guess. Gas, someone said." The old man pursed his lips and shook his head. "I don't trust gas. Never did. Don't like it. One time I had..."

"Anyone hurt?"

He looked at me and frowned. Then he nodded at the left side of the building. "Maybe. Sometimes..."

I didn't hear the rest of his talk. I lasered in on an ambulance parked at the side of the High Tide. I hadn't noticed the vehicle previously. The sick feeling returned to my stomach and a thousand thoughts raced through my mind at once. Shamrock was the first one to work in the morning, but he was still out with a broken ankle. A cook or waitress maybe. Or could it be Dianne? No, not today. I gave myself a mental kick. The ambulance could be just standing by. Funny how I jumped to such a dramatic conclusion. Though maybe it wasn't all that surprising what with everything that'd been happening lately.

The world started to shift as the old anxiety reared its ugly head and I had to step away from the little old man with the big glasses. I took some deep breaths and managed to pull myself together. Over to my right near the curb I noticed a few young women jammed between parked cars. They all wore dark aprons with "High Tide Restaurant & Saloon" emblazoned in white across them. The lunch shift waitresses. I hurried over to them. As soon as they saw me, they all started talking at once.

I focused on what Sylvia, a little older than the other two, was saying. She ran her hand through her kinky blonde hair. "It was horrible. There was an explosion in the kitchen. Dianne was back there. Oh, my god."

Dianne! She usually didn't come in 'til late on Mondays. Then I remembered she'd said she'd be there to see me when I came in. "Jesus, is she all right?"

Sylvia put a hand over her mouth and shook her head. "I dunno, Dan, I dunno. They're taking her away now."

She pointed as the ambulance started to move. The siren and flashers went on. I looked around, desperate to find someone else to talk to. Someone who would tell me that Dianne was all right. Someone to tell me I wasn't to blame.

Chapter 28

"DO YOU WANT a drink?" Steve Moore asked. I shook my head, even though I could have used a double.

We were sitting in a booth at the White Cap Tavern on a side street a couple of blocks from the High Tide. Steve had spotted me in the crowd of onlookers across the street from the High Tide. The fire had been knocked down and had been basically confined to the kitchen; surprisingly, the damage was not extensive. The bad news was that Sylvia had been right—Dianne had been hurt in the explosion. The good news was that Steve had just received a radio call—she was being treated for minor arm burns at Exeter Hospital and it looked like she was going to be okay.

"I want to ask you some questions." Steve had his small notebook on the table between us; he was flicking his pen as usual. "And I want some answers."

"I'll do my best."

A waitress who looked barely old enough to have working papers approached our booth. Steve waved her away. "Time to stop fooling around here, Dan. Are you out of your mind? I told you to knock it off. You don't listen, so you get the shit kicked out of you, then someone tries to blow up the High Tide."

My stomach did a little flip-flop as I got a visual of Dianne in the middle of an explosion. "Someone tried to blow it up?"

"Yeah, that's what we figure. Whoever did it screwed up though. Dianne came in a little early to catch up on what Kelly usually did. By the time their timer went off, she'd closed the jets and aired the place out a lot. Then she called us just before the explosion. It was a lot smaller than it could've been."

"Jesus Christ."

"She was a very lucky woman. She could've been killed."

I let out the breath I was holding. "What kind of maniac would do something like that?"

Steve looked at me with a scowl on his face. "The same kind that used you as a punching bag. Now tell me everything you know."

I could picture poor Dianne on a gurney up at Exeter Hospital. Right about now she probably wished she'd never bought the High Tide from me in the first place. At least it sounded like she was going to be all right.

There was no doubt now I had to be honest with Steve—I was in way over my head. I trusted Steve to do the right thing. Still, I had to keep one bit of information—Kelsey's whereabouts—from him. Steve's right thing might be the wrong thing for Kelsey.

I grabbed the table with both hands. I was sick of repeating my theory, but I wasn't going to give up saying it. "Cora Sweeney was killed, Steve. Murdered. And whoever did it thinks her son is a witness. I've already told you this."

Steve shifted in his seat and gave me a hard look. "I told you if you started nosing around the beach, there might be trouble."

I tried to be reasonable. "And you were right." The young waitress came back. I waved her away this time. "But look. No one would give me a beating like this." I pointed at my face. Steve winced. "Or try to blow up a business with people in it over some little beach Peyton Place thing they didn't want getting around. I'm telling you, someone's got something big to hide. It's gotta be all about Cora Sweeney. Her death wasn't an accident. That's why I got beat and why Kelsey's life is in danger."

Steve sighed and his shoulders sagged a bit. "All right, maybe you do have something. You got any idea who might be responsible?"

"I got a whole bunch of who-might-be-responsibles."

"Names?" He lifted his little notebook off the table.

I took a deep breath and answered. "The boy's father for one."

"Why? They were already divorced, weren't they?"

Steve scribbled as I spoke. "Yeah, but I guess Cora Sweeney got a big insurance settlement. I don't know if they were divorced or going through it or what. But apparently Ober stole the insurance settlement, blew most of the money on dope or something. Anyhow, the judge ordered him to pay the insurance money back in hefty monthly chunks until the entire amount was paid back. Probably would've taken him the rest of his life. Plus, he had child support payments on top of that. That's a motive for murder, isn't it?"

"Maybe. He's a dirtbag, that's for sure. Keep it under your hat, but we've been watching him for a while."

"What for?"

"He's a cook."

"Yeah, but what are you watching him for?"

Steve snorted. "Don't act stupid with me. I know your history."

I just looked at him.

"Crank, Dan. He's cooking crank."

I wasn't being stupid. I was just dense. Meth had never been my drug of choice, but I wasn't ignorant about the drug, either. "Why haven't you grabbed him?"

"We've tried. He moves his little kitchen around quite a bit for a junkie. Every time we think we've got a line on his lab, he changes locations and we have to start all over again. Besides, we think he's small change. We do know somebody big is flooding the entire seacoast right into Massachusetts with meth."

The Ober Sweeney I met had seemed as dumb as a ham sandwich. "Hard to believe he could build a business like that and keep it together."

"That's what we figure too. Besides, he'll probably blow himself up sooner or later anyway. Who else ya got?"

"Mona Freeman, Ober Sweeney's girlfriend. She's a tough woman, Steve, let me tell you. She came to the Tide a day or two before I got snatched and threatened to have me hurt if I didn't leave her boyfriend alone. I also got the impression she thought Ober had still been seeing Cora and she didn't like it. And she sure didn't like him making those monthly payments to Cora."

Steve was still taking notes. "And two days later you got yourself beaten up?"

I took a drink of warm water from a glass on the table. "Yeah. One or two days later. Strange coincidence, huh?"

Steve shrugged. "Anything else?"

"Her landlord was trying to evict her."

"Who was her landlord?"

"Ted Norris. Beautiful Beach Real Estate."

"He's a legitimate beach real estate agent. Been around forever. Why would he want her out that much?"

I leaned across the table. "You know how it works on the beach. The winter people get tossed out so the owners can get the big summer rent from the tourists. And I guess somehow Cora had gotten a year-round lease and maybe Norris didn't like that anymore."

Steve nodded. "Yeah, but even if he kicked her out, he'd probably only make a few extra grand. Not worth killing someone over."

"Tell that to the bank robbers from Charlestown. They'll hit a bank with automatic weapons for no more than that."

Steve shook his head. He waved the young waitress over. She approached with a big smile on her face, a smile that faded when Steve ordered two large Cokes. "You're talking about a businessman, not a hopped-up junkie. Jesus. He's not gonna kill for a few grand unless he's gone off the deep end."

"Maybe he has."

"Ah, now you're grasping. You got anything else?"

I hated to bring the next suspect up because Kelsey was involved, but whatever might be headed his way for a few juvenile B&E's was preferable to being whacked by Bozo. "Well, there is something else — Kelsey was involved in a break or two on the beach. One at Lenny Quarters' place. Lenny supposedly told Cora to get her son to knock it off. I heard he even thought she might be behind the boy doing it."

"Flimsy. That Lenny Land joint is a goldmine." Steve paused and waited for the waitress to set down the drinks and move away from the table. "Jeopardize that because some kid's stealing a few quarters? I don't think so."

"Not just stealing quarters. The machines were broken, too. They probably cost thousands a piece." I pulled the Coke glass closer.

"Again, flimsy. He probably had insurance."

"I don't know about his insurance situation. But I do know one more character that might be involved — Frankie Quail. They call him Frankie Earring. Owns a T-shirt shop on the beach. I guess he's got a bunch of kids ripping-off cottages and stores on the beach for him."

Steve's eyebrows rose. He set down his glass. "That guy's a sleazebag. An ex-con on parole. We know all about him. Matter of fact, we've been keeping an eye on him too. What's the tie-in with the kid and his mother?"

I finally had Steve interested in someone. "Well, Cora heard that Frankie was putting her son up to some breaks and she threatened to turn him into the police. That would have violated his parole and sent him back to prison, right?"

"Maybe. A little more interesting at least. Anyone else?"

I shrugged. "Not that I know of."

We just sat there for a couple of minutes, Steve clicking his pen periodically, me surveying the nautical motif on the walls. I had an idea it was time to push things and Steve had given me an opening with his interest in Frankie Earring. Frankie was as good a start as anyone. I just had to screw up my courage and hope Steve would go for it.

I cleared my throat, stared at Steve.

"I don't like that look you're giving me," he said. "What are you thinking?"

"I was wondering...how much of a sleazebag do you think Frankie Quail is?"

"Big as they come on the beach. The bastard's getting kids involved in crime. Can't go much lower than that. But what are you getting at?"

"Killing two birds with one stone. You might get rid of a Fagin-like character, and at the same time, get to the bottom of what we've been talking about. Are you game?"

Steve frowned. "Within reason. What do you have in mind?"

I told him my idea.

"You think that'll get us anywhere?" Steve asked.

"It might. It'll definitely put the brakes on his kid crime ring. All you have to do is control the patrol cars for a couple hours."

Steve snorted. "You're asking a lot, Sherlock. Frankie Earring's not too popular down the station but I'll have to dodge the chief and Gant, my direct superior. And you'd have to keep your mouth shut about my involvement."

"You've got my word."

Steve studied my face for a moment, then said, "All right. When?"

"Soon. If you give me your number, I'll call."

He took out his wallet, removed a business card, and slid it across the table to me. "And now what about the kid?"

I didn't look at Steve as I answered, "I don't know where he is."

"You sure about that?"

"I'm sure." Out of the side window I could see a couple of reporters and a cameraman heading up toward Ocean Boulevard, most likely to the High Tide.

"All right." Steve glanced out the window and grimaced. "I better get out there before they start bothering people too much. Talk to you later."

He was probably hoping for an interview himself. I held up my hand, said, "Okay."

Steve jammed the notebook into his shirt pocket along with the pen, popped on his mirrored shades, and strode out of the White Cap. The young waitress dropped off the check for two Cokes. It was only a few bucks, but because we'd tied up a table, I left her a ten.

I knew the Tide wouldn't be open for at least today and there were a couple of things I had to take care of, so I decided to make a stop before heading home. It would be a lot different from where I sat now—night and day. My next destination was a biker bar to see my old friend Tiny. And with Tiny anything could happen. Except dying of boredom.

Chapter 29

WALLY'S IS A BIKER BAR that'd been on the beach a long time. It was a standard biker bar—lots of motorcycles, long hair, beards, and leather. What wasn't standard was its friendliness. You didn't have to be a biker to go in there and feel comfortable. Lots of non-bikers did. I never heard of anyone ever being hassled there because they weren't part of the biker culture. I'd been there dozens of times through the years and had never gotten a hard look or had fighting words thrown my way. And believe me, a lot of those times I'd probably deserved more than that. It was another place on the beach I'd closed many a night. So I had a soft spot for Wally's. Besides, they had great pizza and cold beer.

It was just after noon when I got there and already there was a collection of Harleys parked along the side of the building. Not near as many as there would be later in the day but it was a good start. I was hoping the man I was coming to see was here this early. I needn't have worried because I didn't even have to step inside the bar to find him. He found me.

Outside, behind a metal railing, sat a group of tables and chairs for patrons to use during nice weather. Today was one of those days. A few of the tables were already occupied.

"Dan. Dan Marlowe." The voice reverberated across the patio. The speaker was sitting alone at a corner table where he could survey Ashworth Avenue.

"Hey, Tiny." I walked through the opening in the railing and approached the big man's table. Tiny Dancer. It was a nickname he'd picked up somewhere along the way. Of course, no one ever called him that to his face. I mean the Dancer part. It was just "Tiny." We were close back during a time I've forgotten a lot about. And that's not a bad thing. Convenient amnesia.

As I approached, Tiny put his bottle of Bud down, got up, came around the table and gave me a bear hug. And I mean a bear hug. The man had a few inches on me and had to weigh close to 300 pounds. It wasn't all fat and it wasn't all muscle, but whatever it was you didn't want to screw with it.

"Brother, what the hell you been doin'?" He slapped my back and I had to struggle to stay on my feet. I returned the slap and felt like I'd just smacked a stone wall.

"I'm still up the Tide, Tiny. Just the bartender now."

"Yeah, I heard. Well, at least you still got your ass in the old joint. Me, I don't get up that way much. More comfortable down here." He pulled a chair out for me and sat heavily back on his own chair.

Tiny hadn't changed much since the last time I'd spoken to him. I'd seen him off and on through the years, either holding court here at Wally's outside in nice weather, or I'd catch a glimpse of his big frame through the plate glass window when the weather was bad. He still wore his black hair in a ponytail but I detected some new streaks of gray. Ditto for his full beard. He had on jeans, boots, a black T-shirt, and a leather vest. It was the only way I could remember Tiny ever being dressed.

"You still drinking that Kraut shit?" Tiny asked. Before I could answer he called to a barmaid delivering drinks a few tables over. "Hey, Evie. Another one for me and a Heineken for my buddy."

"Wait your turn, Tiny."

"You gonna embarrass me in front of my friend, wench?"

As the barmaid went back inside she jokingly stuck out her tongue.

"They love me here," Tiny said, taking a pull on his beer.

Before we had time to exchange more than the typical pleasantries, she was back with the beers and a glass for me. "There you go, Mr. Dancer."

Tiny laughed and reached out for her waist. "You're lucky I like you." Apparently some things had changed.

The barmaid twirled and walked away. Before she got inside she said, "You're lucky we like you. Who else'd have you?"

"She's got a point there." Tiny crossed thick tattooed forearms on the table. "Well, what the hell's up? Figure it must have something to do with the fire up at the Tide. Ain't seen you in...shit...I don't know how long."

I took a sip of the Heineken. Icy cold, just how I liked it. "Has to do with the fire, but that's not the whole story. Dianne was hurt, but she's okay." Tiny had a history with Dianne too. She pulled our collective bacon out of the fire a few times years ago when we'd both been going wild on the beach.

"Jesus Christ. She try to put it out or something? Get burned? She always had a lot of balls."

I didn't really like telling Tiny all this but I had to find out if there was any connection between what I was involved in and what happened to Dianne. She had told me she wouldn't speak to Tiny but I had the sickening feeling that possibly she had. And if she had, maybe that's why someone made a move on her. If I was lucky, Tiny was going to tell me he hadn't seen her and then I'd at least be able to shake the cloud of guilt that was forming in my mind, the cloud that held the little voice that kept whispering I was the cause of harm to someone I cared for.

"It wasn't actually a fire, Tiny. It was an explosion. Maybe not an accident."

I saw something I'd never seen before on his face — shock. The look slowly subsided and was replaced by something I was more familiar with seeing there — red rage. "Those fuckin' bastards. I'll kick their asses." And I believed he might, whoever they were.

"So you've seen her recently."

He took another long pull on his beer and eyeballed me. "Well, she told me not to say anything if I saw ya. But yeah, she was here a couple a days ago. Told me what happened to ya." He pointed the beer bottle at my face. "The chick was worried about you, Dan. Told me the story and a few names. Asked me if I'd tell 'em to keep their hands off you. I couldn't say no to Dianne. I owe her. We both do."

Yes, we did. She'd done everything for us, from bailing us out of jail, to letting us crash at her place for a couple of days. And we weren't fun characters to be around then either. I wouldn't have wanted to be around us myself. Anyhow, I figured I'd at least get to find out who Tiny spoke to and that would give me a line on who was behind all this.

"So who did you speak to?" I asked.

Tiny cocked his head. "Well, I told one of the Seabrookers to tell that skinny little shit, Sweeney, to mind his manners or I'd come over and break his hands. Fuckin' crank head."

Ober Sweeney. It had to be him then. I was in luck. But only 'til Tiny spoke again.

"Then I took a walk up the beach and saw that fat fuck Lenny Quarters. I dropped in on Frankie Earring's shirt joint too. Damn fag. I warned them. Now somebody's gonna pay."

So I was back to square one. The only suspects on my list he hadn't mentioned were Mona Freeman and Ted Norris. Freeman would've heard from her boyfriend and Norris was a real estate agent, for God's sake. Agents know if someone's got their bathing suit on backwards on the beach. Everyone I was suspicious of knew that Dianne was involved now. It could've been any one of them.

I'd opened this can of worms with Tiny but now I had to close it. Quick. The man was like a burning stick of dynamite and just as lethal. I'd seen him in action. Time to use my ace. "Tiny, I have to ask you a favor."

"I gotta feelin' I know what it is. But for you, Dan, anything. Almost."

"Can you stay out of this for a while? Not mention any of this to anybody?"

The way Tiny looked you'd think I was asking him to give up his Harley. He leaned across the table until I could smell the beer on his breath. I didn't dare back away. "Dan, one a those fuckin' assholes hurt Dianne. And I ain't no dunce. I figure it was probably my fault. I'm gonna break somebody's head." He sat back in his chair. Looked at me hard.

Tiny on a rampage would only make things a lot worse. "Look, Dianne's going to be all right. Those people already knew she was involved. You didn't stir things up any more than they were already stirred up. Besides, there are other people who could've done this." Back-to-back lies, that was a first even for me. "I'm going to get to the bottom of this. The cops are involved too. So if you could just let us handle it, you have my promise — someone'll pay."

If I thought the word "cops" was going to scare Tiny, I must've been tripping. He crossed those big arms across his massive chest. "That ain't the way it works, Dan. I went to see 'em, told 'em to lay off you and don't bother Dianne either. Jackass me. Shouldn't have even mentioned her name. That's why it's my fault and that's why somebody's gonna get whaled on. Besides, nobody shits on me."

Jesus! If I didn't figure out how to sidetrack him, Tiny could end up hospitalizing half of Hampton Beach. "How about this — you let me keep digging around. I'm sure I can find out who did this. If I can't get the cops to nail whoever's responsible on a big-time charge, I'll turn any names over to you and you can handle it in your own way." Tiny didn't answer, so I tried another ploy. "People know your rep, Tiny. If they think you're after them, they'll hijack an Al Gauron party boat to get out of the country. We'll never get them then."

He studied me for a long minute. "Okay, bro. But the cops don't bust the jerk behind it and give him heavy time, I want the name. Understood?"

"Understood." I'd lucked out. Now was the perfect time to mention the other reason I'd come to see Tiny. I told him what I had in mind. It was like throwing a bone to a wild animal.

Tiny looked at me quizzically. "And you say I won't get any heat for it?"

"You got my word."

Tiny leaned back and the chair groaned. "Well, I don't know how the hell you're gonna do it but your word's good enough for me. When?"

"Tomorrow too soon?"

A smile crossed his face. "Of course not. This is gonna be fun."

We went over a couple more things, and then I decided it was time to change the subject. "Another beer, Tiny?"

He let out a laugh that would have scared anyone who didn't know him. "Stupid question, Dan. We got a lot of catching up to do." Tiny turned toward the barmaid just passing our table. "Wench, two more, please."

She glanced our way. "Gee, that's a surprise. I thought that mighta been your last for the day."

"Funny, Evie. I'll remember that when it's tip time."

"When it's tip time you won't be able to remember anything. Especially anything as little as that."

Tiny raised his bottle to his mouth, drained it, and thumped the empty bottle down on the table. "I told ya, Dan. They love me here."

I believed they did.

I would have liked to sit and reminisce with Tiny all day. And I was sure he would have liked it if we ended up closing Wally's like we often did in the old days. But I was worried about Kelsey. So I had a couple more beers, and after what seemed like enough time had passed so Tiny wouldn't be too offended, I excused myself. As I got up to leave, Tiny gave me one of his signature bear hugs and almost cracked my spine.

I walked quickly home, imagining a rogue's gallery of dangerous characters that could have shown up at the cottage in my absence. I prayed none of them had.

Chapter 30

WHEN I GOT HOME, I found that Kelsey was all right. There was only one surprise waiting for me—a message on my answering machine. I hit the play button and heard a cold, gravelly voice. "Last time, Marlowe. Retire from the detective racket or the next time we'll blow the place up with you in it." Kelsey hadn't heard the message and I didn't tell him about it either.

Early the next morning I reluctantly left Kelsey alone in the cottage with a few videos I'd picked up for him. Once in my car I loaded the revolver, left it on the seat beside me. I removed one of the Xanax tabs from the prescription bottle and let it dissolve under my tongue. Then I headed for a little dirt road over in Seabrook.

During the drive I couldn't shake the thought of Dianne caught in that explosion and of how things could have turned out. She was lucky; I was lucky. It could just as easily have been me caught in that blast. Thank god Dianne was going to be all right. But it was my fault. Retaliation for my activities. I had to set it right.

And I had to do it before anyone else was hurt.

I didn't know what I was going to do when I got to Sweeney's. Revenge wasn't really my style, although it probably would have felt good right about then. But revenge wasn't important. I had to do something before someone else was killed. That was important. So I was going to shake things up. No matter what happened, I had to be ready — and get whatever was going to happen over with quickly.

I couldn't be certain if either Ober Sweeney or Mona Freeman was involved in Cora Sweeney's death or the explosion at the Tide. But the odds were with me. There were five possible suspects that I knew about, and in about five minutes I was going to confront two of them.

By the time I pulled up to the rundown house trailer the Xanax had kicked in and I felt calm as a rock. The property didn't seem quite so dismal as the last time I'd been there. Maybe I was getting used to it. Then again, maybe it was just the pill. I climbed out of the car, tucked the gun in the rear waistband of my jeans and pulled my shirt tail down over it. I walked up and pounded on the trailer door.

The door opened before I could knock again and there stood Ober Sweeney, looking like a sack-a-shit as usual. His facial tics hadn't slowed down any since the last time I'd seen him. He seemed surprised for a second to see me and then quickly recovered. "I thought I told you to stay the fuck away from here."

"I want to talk to you again."

"Who is it, O?"

Before he could answer, Mona Freeman's dilapidated face peered over his shoulder. When she saw me, she let loose with a barrage of obscenities, spittle flying from her mouth.

"I wanna talk to you again too," I said.

"Fuck you," Mona screamed. She disappeared for a couple of seconds and then she was back, trying to get around Sweeney, a large wicked-looking carving knife in her hand. Sweeney blocked the door, but it didn't look like he was trying too hard to stop her. I whipped out the .38 and jabbed the barrel deep into Sweeney's skinny gut. His eyes popped wide open. Mona was still trying to get around him and at me.

"Stop it, you stupid bitch," Sweeney said over his shoulder. "He's got a piece in my belly."

Mona flailed her arms a bit more, but she stopped trying to get to me with the carving knife.

"Back up and get inside, both of you." I shoved the revolver harder into Sweeney's belly. "And throw that knife on the floor."

Ober Sweeney looked genuinely terrified, like his cranked-up heart might finally give out. Mona gave me a stare as menacing as the knife. They both backed up and she tossed the turkey shaver on the floor. I followed them into the trailer. It smelled like a flop house room in the old Boston Combat Zone — cigarette butts, stale beer, and that strange sickeningly-sweet body odor methedrine addicts emit.

"Sit." I waved my free hand at a stained couch and kept the revolver on them until they were both settled.

I stood over them, staying just out of their reach. Mona glared up at me defiantly. Sweeney had completely fallen apart. He couldn't take his eyes off the revolver in my hand. He must've taken some speed just before I arrived. It wasn't possible for a person to make the bizarre facial movements he was making without massive — recent — artificial stimulation.

"I'm here about the fire at the High Tide Monday," I said, looking at Sweeney first, then Mona. "You almost killed someone over there, you shitheads. Could've burnt the place down."

Mona almost jumped out of her chair at me; only the gun stopped her. "If it was a friend a yours, good. Too bad it wasn't you."

Sweeney held up his hands. "Whoa, whoa, man," he said, voice cracking. "I didn't have nothin' to do with hurtin' nobody, no way. I was here all day Monday."

"You could've set your little surprise Sunday night."

"I don't know what you're talking about, but I was here then too. I was...ahh...well, I was here."

"What about her?" I waved the gun barrel at Mona.

"We was both here. Weren't we, baby?" Sweeney looked at Mona.

Mona crossed her scrawny arms across her chest. "I'm tellin' him zero."

Sweeney raised his hand like he was going to back-hand her. "Don't screw around, bitch. He's got a gun. Tell him we was here."

Mona looked at me like she was going to spit, but instead she said, "We haven't been outta here for the past three days."

The way they were both jacked-up, I believed that was possible. "What about your two friends—Reagan and Bozo? The two that worked me over. You could've sent them to rig the explosion."

"What friends you talkin' about?" Sweeney said. "We ain't got no damn friends."

I could believe that, too. "The ones your girlfriend there threatened to sic on me."

Sweeney glared at Mona. "What's he talkin' about?"

"I told him to stop bothering you or I'd have some-body kick his ass."

"You went to see him?" Sweeney asked. "You threat-ened him?"

"Yeah. I didn't want him hasslin' you. And I didn't tell nobody to bother him or his friend."

"You stupid shit. So that's why he's here again. You coulda screwed up..." Sweeney stopped short. He drew back his hand like he was going to smack her and she balled her fists like she was going to give it right back.

I waved the gun at them. "Knock it off, you morons. I'm not here to watch you two fight." They both glanced at the gun in my hand and backed off reluctantly. "What about the night your ex-wife was killed, Sweeney? Where were you two that night?"

He got a little indignant. "What difference does it make? I told you the stupid whore killed herself."

"And I'm asking you where you were when she died?" I poked the gun at him and he suddenly lost his indignation.

"What night was it?" he asked.

"You know what night it was."

Sweeney threw his hands up. "It was weeks ago. How the hell can I remember what I was doing way back then?"

He had a point; after all, he didn't have much of a brain left to work with. "What about you?" I nodded at Mona.

"How the hell should I know?"

"How 'bout both of you think about this — I told the cops about you not wanting to pay your ex back that insurance settlement you swiped. They're probably thinking right about now that money is a pretty good motive for murder."

Sweeney looked like his bowels had loosened. "How did you know about that?"

I decided to toss some gas on the fire. "She told me." I grinned at Mona. Maybe revenge wasn't my thing, but it sure was sweet.

Sweeney turned on her. "You stupid fuckin' bitch. The cops'll think I killed her. Puttin' ideas in their heads. I oughta kill you."

Mona sprang like a wild cat, jumping on him and scratching at his eyes. Sweeney yelled, grabbed a fistful of her greasy hair and pulled hard.

"You try it, you cocksucker," Mona screamed. "I'll kill you first."

I'd had enough of them both. Besides, I didn't need more on my conscience than I already had. I took a couple of steps toward them and jabbed the gun twice into the side of Sweeney's head. "All right. Break it up, break it up."

Seemed like Sweeney was trying to back off, but Mona was still a spitfire, scratching at his face and doing a good job of it.

I decided to stop her before she scarred him more than he already was. I turned the gun on her. "Leave him alone or I'll smash this across your puss."

That worked. She pulled away, panting hard like an overheated dog, eyes blazing. Sweeney gently touched his face, probably making sure both eyes were still there. Both cheeks had deep bloody gouges.

When they both looked like they'd calmed down enough to understand me I said, "I'm leaving now, but I got something I want to tell you before I go."

Sweeney swiped at a stream of blood running down his thin pockmarked face. "Look, neither of us killed Cora or torched the High Tide. Anything this stupid bitch said was just talk. She was tryin' to scare you is all."

"Stupid bitch?" Mona shouted. "I didn't tell him shit."

It would have started all over again.

"Shut the hell up, both of you. Now."

They quieted right down, glaring at me like two wild animals. Now I knew how lion tamers felt. "Like I told you...the cops know all about you two having a reason to want Cora dead." I nodded toward Mona. "And about the threats you made too. So if anything happens to me, those same cops are going to come looking for you both. And whether you're guilty or not, I figure you wouldn't want the police traipsing around here. I think they'd kind of cramp your lifestyle, don't you?"

They both just sat there. Mona sullen, as usual; Sweeney scared, his tics moving like a nest of worms under his skin. Neither of them made a peep. I added one more thing before I turned to leave. "If any harm comes to Kelsey..." I had to force myself to say the next two words, "...your son, I won't call the police. I'll come back here and kill you both. Nobody's going to care about two dead speed freaks in a shithole of a trailer with bullets in their heads."

On the drive back to Hampton I started shaking. I wasn't shaking from anxiety — not after taking that pill — I was shaking from good old-fashioned excitement. I wasn't sure if I'd accomplished anything but I was glad I'd stood up to the pair nonetheless. If nothing else, those two would probably think twice before making a move against me or Kelsey.

If Sweeney and his sleep mate hadn't been behind all the trouble — and I still wasn't sure of their innocence — then who? Someone was trying to get to the boy and me. There'd been enough carnage to prove that. I had to flush out whoever was behind this mess and get this damn thing over with quick. After all, I could only play the tough guy for so long.

Chapter 31

AFTER I RETURNED to the cottage, dropped my car off, and checked on Kelsey, I took a walk up Ocean Boulevard on the beach side. I had an appointment to see the little entertainment I'd arranged. The weather was great—not a cloud visible and hot for late May. Those ingredients brought out an early beach crowd. The sand was littered with almost as many blankets as a weekday in July. The crowd would work in favor of what I hoped was about to unfold.

When I reached my destination, I sat up on the beach railing, my back to the Atlantic. I focused on the business directly across Ocean Boulevard from me—Frankie's T-Shirt Shop. The overhead garage-like doors were rolled open and the entire front of the shop was exposed. Inside, the store was crowded already, with day-trippers rifling the racks of shirts and ogling the risqué transfers plastered on the walls. There was a steady stream of people in and out.

I kept an eye on Frankie's as well as the pedestrian traffic passing by. Young people, old people, couples and singles. A rollerblader came flying down the boardwalk, dodging people as she went and scaring more than a few of the older ones along the way. Throngs of teenagers bumping into each other and laughing, skipping school their big adventure for the year. All out for the first nice promise of summer, and all sporting the pasty-white skin of another long New England winter.

A roar reverberated through the air from the direction of a one-way side street that led up from Ashworth Avenue. I looked toward the noise as a procession of Harleys rounded the corner onto Ocean Boulevard, headed in my direction. I smiled as more than a half-dozen of the motorcyclists pulled up across the street from me and maneuvered their bikes, backing them into a tight line at the curb with their tailpipes aimed directly at Frankie's wide-open shop. The narrow sidewalk was all that separated the machines from the exposed business. The bikers gunned their engines. My eardrums vibrated, and it only took a couple of minutes before exhaust fumes drifted across the boulevard to sting my nose.

It wasn't long before Frankie emerged from the store and saw what and who he was dealing with. He waved his arms and shouted something I had no hope of making out over the distance and the noise. Too bad I couldn't read lips. Then again, I didn't really need to.

Frankie was being totally ignored by Tiny and his friends. He finally threw up his hands, turned, and ran back into his shop passing customers running out. Some of them were covering their ears, others coughing, some both.

It was my turn now. I hopped off the railing and strolled across Ocean Boulevard, giving Tiny a sly wink as I passed. He nodded and I walked into the T-shirt shop.

I found Frankie Earring in the back of the shop behind a glass display case. He had one hand on a heat transfer machine while the other hand plastered a phone to his ear. He was yelling into the phone; I wasn't sure if it was because he was angry or because of the racket from the bikes. Probably both. I watched as he pressed his free hand to his other ear, yelled some more, and slammed the phone down.

He noticed me for the first time and looked a bit taken aback. "Marlowe. What the hell do you want?"

I had to shout above the din. "Thought you might need some help, Frankie." I nodded in the direction of the bikes. "Maybe a little tit for tat."

"I don't need no damn help." He rubbed his gold earring between thumb and forefinger. The earring was tarnished. "I juth called the cops."

"Well, if you change your mind..."

"What are you talking about? Get outta my way." He came around the display case and headed for the front of the store. I noticed his T-shirt read, *Amateur Gynecologist*, as he brushed past me.

He stopped at the entrance, just inside the now-empty shop. He had his hands on his hips, staring at the bikers. I sauntered up and stood beside him. I could see his eyes watering, mine were too. The fumes being blasted into the store were overpowering. We both coughed continuously.

Frankie suddenly dropped his arms and said, "Here we go."

He smiled and pointed at an approaching Hampton police cruiser. The cruiser slowly slid past us, the two cops inside facing straight ahead. The noise of the bikes was still ear-splitting. Frankie and I watched the cruiser go on its merry way up Ocean Boulevard. I wasn't surprised. *Thank you, Steve Moore.*

Frankie was plenty surprised though. He took three steps out to the sidewalk; I followed. "Hey..." Frankie began, then broke into a fit of sputtering coughs, waving his arms in the direction of the disappearing police car. "What the...?" he finally squeaked.

"Want that help now, Frankie?" I said, wiping tears from my eyes.

He looked at me. His eyes were on fire from anger and exhaust fumes. "Marlowe," he growled. "You're behind thith. I should have known."

He turned and stormed into the deserted store with me right behind him. He stalked to the rear of the store and threw open a door marked "Office." I followed him inside. I knew I had him then. No beach business owner with half a brain would leave his store open and unattended for even a minute for fear that shoplifters would strike. Unless of course they assumed that no one, shoplifters included, was apt to venture into an ear-piercing gas chamber.

Frankie sat down behind a scarred metal desk, banged it hard with his fist. He cleared his throat and spoke. "All right, Marlowe," he squeaked and cleared his throat again. "What do you want?"

"Well, Frankie, old boy," I said, starting to really enjoy this now. "You can start by giving me names. Unless you want a motorcycle rally outside your shop every day for the rest of the summer. And you know which names I'm looking for."

Frankie Earring glared at me like he was debating whether to get physical or not. I almost wished he would, but whether it was me or the fear of the bikers out front, he chose not to.

"I don't know what you're talking about, Marlowe."

"I can leave now if that's the way you want to play it, Frankie." I turned and reached for the door knob.

Frankie held up a hand. "Whoa, whoa, whoa. I didn't thay that. Like I told you before—I don't know nothing. Thtill, I do know a lot of people on the beach. Maybe I could come up with thomething. I'm well rethpected around here after all."

Frankie noticed my double take on that last statement. He turned away from my gaze and started rubbing his earring furiously.

"Yeah, you're a regular Rotarian, Frankie. But you better give me some names fast. If not..." I turned in the direction of the roaring motorcycles and hacked. I didn't have to fake it either. The noxious fumes had leaked under the door and into the office. Once I could speak again I added, "And Frankie, anything happens to Kelsey or any of my friends, I'm going to assume it was you behind it and those boys outside won't stay on their bikes next time they come around." I smiled.

Frankie didn't like that. "Get out, Marlowe."

I gave him the finger, left the office, and hurried through the shop as fast as I could. The fumes were so thick it looked like an early morning fog had drifted into the building. I held my breath until I stepped outside.

Tiny and his buddies were still straddled on their bikes revving the engines. Pedestrians walked out onto Ocean Boulevard where they could get past the bikes without getting fumigated quite as badly as on the sidewalk. I nodded to Tiny. He threw me a peace sign, signaled his pals. They gunned their engines one last time and pulled out, zipping around traffic on their way up Ocean. I watched until they were out of sight. Then I dodged across the street and started walking south.

The fresh salt air felt good in my lungs; they'd taken a beating in Frankie Earring's T-Shirt Shop. But it had been worth it. Frankie was a long-time beach weasel and everyone knows weasels aren't big on courage. I was pretty sure Frankie would make some panicked move. In fact, I was counting on it. I just didn't know what that move would be.

Chapter 32

WEDNESDAY MORNING things were back to a slow pace again on the beach. Dianne had called last night to let me know the Tide was reopening. I wasn't too surprised; she didn't like losing business. The holiday weekend was behind us and the beach had entered that lull period in activity that would run until the last week in June when things would pick up again. A great time to be on the beach, one of my favorite times of the year. The weather was usually pleasant and there were no crowds.

Although today the weather wasn't cooperating. I was driving to work for a change. Rain beat against the windshield, my wipers were on high, and the ocean was a churning black mass.

When I got to the High Tide I parked across the street in one of the spots Dianne leased. I got soaked making the short dash across the street and around the building to the back door. I let myself in and walked into the kitchen.

Dianne hadn't wasted any time getting the place back together. She'd been released from the hospital the day of the explosion and had gotten one of those disaster repair companies in immediately, along with a couple of beach handymen she always used. Everybody worked around the clock. I had to admit they'd done a hell of a job. Except for some scorched areas above the stove where the explosion took place, you wouldn't know anything had happened. I stopped for a minute and stared, then shivered. Just looking at that scorch mark gave me the willies. I shook my head and headed out front. The dining room and bar area looked fine.

I'd been hoping to see Dianne, but it appeared she'd already come and gone. Not unusual for her even under normal circumstances. She'd often come in early for a few hours, take off, and then come back again for the night shift. I'd talked to her on the phone since the explosion, but was still anxious to talk to her face to face. I needed to apologize...again.

Explosions in Hampton Beach were unusual and the High Tide had been on the news and in newspapers, even the two Boston rags. Everyone would be talking about the incident today—waitresses, regulars, even the not-so-regulars—and I didn't look forward to the talk. I had some things I wanted to look into and I couldn't if I started dwelling on Dianne and all the what-might-have-beens.

The first thing on my list was to check in on Ted Norris. I hadn't noticed the real estate agent at the scene of Cora Sweeney's cottage explosion. Usually a beach landlord, especially one plugged in like Norris, would be on location before the fire trucks. I walked over to the pay phone on the wall, looked up the number for Beautiful Beach Real Estate. I dropped in silver and dialed. On the second ring a woman answered.

"Beautiful Beach Real Estate."

"I'm interested in buying a piece of property," I said. The woman started to quiz me but I interrupted her. "I know the lot I'd like. It's Number Twenty Reed Street on the beach." She excused herself, but was back in a minute to tell me the property was unavailable. They had other lots for sale, though.

"Well, I like that lot," I pushed. "That's the only one I'm interested in."

Her voice cracked when she told me again it was unavailable.

"Why? What's the problem?" I asked, trying to sound indignant.

"No problem, sir."

"I figured after what happened there, the lot would be available. By the way what exactly did happen there?"

She ignored the question. "Now sir, I have..."

I interrupted her again. "I'm interested in that lot and I'm willing to pay."

She hemmed and hawed and I could hear a man giving her instructions in the background. Probably Norris.

I tried one more tack. One that would tempt any property owner on the beach. "I'm open as far as price goes."

For the third time, she told me the property was unavailable. She tried again to interest me in others, but I quickly blew her off and said good-bye.

I headed behind the bar and started setting up. Why wouldn't Cora Sweeney's lot be up for sale? Especially with a buyer who said he had a fat wallet and would open it wide. And the woman hadn't mentioned the explosion. Why the mystery? I'd known the first time I'd met Norris that he didn't leave any coins lying on his floor. So why no interest in an open-ended offer? What was up? It didn't make any sense.

The situation wasn't any clearer a short time later when Steve Moore came through the front door and took a stool at the bar. He looked tired and removed his shades like they were very heavy. Why he bothered with sunglasses with all the rain outside was beyond me. Maybe it was just habit.

We exchanged pleasantries and then he got down to business. "Your little trick worked, Sherlock."

I could see that he was waiting for me to say something and wasn't going to tell me anything unless I did. "What happened?"

"Frankie Quail didn't waste any time. We had the place under surveillance. He closed up his shop right after you and your biker friends left. We trailed him to his apartment on L Street. He threw a couple of suitcases in his car and we followed him over the Hampton Bridge. We had the Salisbury cops grab him when he crossed into Massachusetts. That's a parole violation without his PO's permission."

My first customer of the day came in—he was an old-timer, a regular. I excused myself, greeted the man, and without asking, poured him a draft Bud and put an order in the kitchen for baked haddock, mashed, and vegetables. I set his place with bread, silverware, napkin, salt, pepper, and returned to Steve. "What did he tell you?"

"What'd he tell me? He talked so much we had to stuff a sock in his mouth to shut him up. I figured an ex-con like that would be a little tougher. He crumbled like a stale cookie. Not that what he told us was what you were hoping for."

"You didn't get anything helpful out of him?"

"Some minor stuff."

"And Cora Sweeney?"

Steve gave me a disapproving look. "There's probably nothing to tell there. Her death is still ruled accidental."

I tried not to get angry. "Look, Steve, I really believe everything that's happened—the explosions, my beating, someone trying to snatch Kelsey, not to mention what happened to Shamrock and Guillermo—all ties back to Cora Sweeney. If her death wasn't murder, I'll eat all the seaweed on Hampton Beach."

"You better get a fork and knife ready. Look, gimme a Coke."

I got Steve his Coke and dropped the baked haddock off at the other end of the bar. Then I came back to Steve. "Well, if all this isn't about Cora, what the hell is it about?"

Steve gave me a sly look. "Another friend of yours. Lenny Conklin. I guess most of the stuff Frankie was having the kids steal for him was going to Conklin. VCR's, TV's, jewelry, stuff like that. Mostly from beach places but even a few estates up in North Hampton and Rye. Conklin supposedly has some good outs for hot goods down in Massachusetts."

Interesting. "Did you find a tie-in with Cora Sweeney?"

Steve took a drink, then shook his head. "There is none."

"Are you sure?"

"I told you this guy was about as stand up as a washed-up boxer. If there was any connection, we would have found it. Quail would've flipped on his mother, for Chrissake. We got a parole violation on him and he does not want to go back in. I'm surprised he made it through his first stint. He a fag or something, the way he talks?"

I rolled my eyes. "I dunno. He's got a lisp, I guess."

"I guess he does."

"So why was he taking off?"

Steve grinned. "You'll get a kick out of this. Says a bartender on the strip was threatening him about Cora Sweeney's death and he got scared."

"Of me?"

"Well, the bikers probably had something to do with it, too. There was something else. I probably shouldn't tell you this because you'll make more of it than it is, but Lenny Conklin had Frankie get Kelsey Sweeney to break into his arcade."

A couple of customers, fishermen by their looks, sauntered into the bar and I had to tear myself away from Steve to wait on them. I was a little short with them and they told me so. I couldn't blame them. When I'd finished putting in their orders, I returned to Steve. "Why the hell would Conklin want the boy to break into his own arcade?"

"The goofball didn't know. But it was set up so Quarters would catch the kid in the act. Frankie didn't know what happened after that."

The lunch crowd started pouring in and I had to excuse myself again. Steve caught my arm. "Still haven't seen the kid, Dan?"

I hated lying to him but nothing Steve said had convinced me that Kelsey was in any less danger than he had been before. "No, I haven't."

I watched the customers plopping themselves down along the length of the bar and acted like I was anxious to get to them, which I was—for more than one reason. Steve gave me a quizzical look and for a second I was sure he knew where Kelsey was. Out of the corner of my eye, I could see him studying me as I waited on the lunch gang.

Chapter 33

AFTER STEVE LEFT I couldn't wait for my shift to end. I wasn't sure what to make of Lenny Quarters setting up Kelsey to be caught breaking into his arcade. It probably would have been wise not to do anything until I had a better idea of what was going on, but I didn't have time to be wise. The more time that passed before this thing was squared away, the more chance that someone else would turn up dead. So I decided to stir things up again; see if someone else would make a mistake.

The clock hands moved like the proverbial snail even though I was as busy as a one-armed paper hanger. Finally the shift was over. The rain had stopped and I made a beeline for my car. I drove directly to Lenny Land and parked across the street. Once again, I grabbed my gun from the glove box, shoved it in the rear of my waistband, and pulled my shirt free to conceal it. I walked across Ocean Boulevard and into Lenny Land.

As usual the place was all noise and motion, bells and whistles and youngsters moving about. I saw the same geek with the standard purple shirt I'd seen before, but this time I walked right through the arcade and marched up to the door marked "Office." I reached behind my back and adjusted the .38, reassuring myself the gun was still there. Then I knocked on the door and walked in.

Fat Lenny Conklin, with the bald head and the purple shirt, was sitting behind his desk just like the last time I'd seen him. The room stank of garlic. He looked surprised to see me, and maybe a little frightened, but he didn't waste any time. "What the hell do you want?"

There was no time to feel anxious. "I want to talk to you, Conklin."

He looked at me like I was dirt under his feet. "I ain't got time. I'm countin' my money."

He didn't look like he was counting money to me. He did have a few sacks full of coins open on the floor beside his desk, but I knew those would have to be either weighed or run through a coin-counting machine. Probably just being cute. "I don't care whether you've got time or not. You're going to talk to me and you're going to like it."

Suddenly, Conklin didn't look so cocky.

"Why did you set Kelsey Sweeney up so you could catch him breaking into this arcade?"

One look at his face and I knew Frankie Earring had told the truth.

Conklin's fat face reddened and he leaned across the desk toward me. "I don't know what you're talking about. I didn't set that little shit up for anything."

"Frankie Quail's telling the police different. He's also telling them about your fencing operation. You two are real sweethearts, using kids in something like that."

Beads of sweat popped out on his shiny forehead and his eyes darted around like he might be thinking about making a break for it. "I don't know what you're talkin' about. Frankie Quail...he's crazy. I didn't do nothin' to that kid."

"And his mother?"

I stepped forward, put my hands on his desk, and leaned into his face. I drew back a bit when he opened his mouth. Talk about garlic. "His mother? I didn't have nothin' to do with his mother. Nobody's gonna pin that on me."

"That isn't what Frankie says," I lied.

He waved his hand. "He's a dirty liar." Then he hesitated and started again. "And I ain't gonna talk to you no more neither. You ain't a cop. You're just a fuckin' bartender. Now get the fuck outta here." He pointed his finger gun-style at the door.

I pulled the real thing from behind my back and Lenny looked like he was going to have a heart attack right then and there. I didn't point the .38 at him, just held the revolver down by my side. "I'm going to find out one way or another who killed Cora Sweeney, Conklin.

I think you might've murdered her and I'm going to do everything I can to convince the cops of that. And when I do, they'll grill you good. Unless I hear you tell me something that changes my mind."

Whether or not Conklin was the killer, I wanted whoever was behind the beating I'd taken to know if they came after me again, it wasn't going to be so easy the second time around. I wanted him and the others to know the stakes had been raised—I wasn't the only one who might get hurt.

He shook his head rapidly, flinging sweat in all directions. "I didn't kill nobody. Nobody, I tell ya."

"Sure you didn't. And there isn't any sand on Hampton Beach either." I tucked the .38 back in my waistband and tugged my shirt over it. Then I gave Lenny Quarters a disdainful look, turned, and walked out of his office. I walked through the arcade and back to my car across the street.

I sat in my car, eyes glued to the front of Lenny Land. Only about five minutes passed before I saw Conklin come out, cross the street, and hop into a Caddy parked at the curb. I followed as he drove north on Ocean Boulevard. I stayed a couple of cars behind him as we went by the Casino, the Ashworth Hotel, and up as far as Boar's Head before he made a U-turn and came around, heading south on Ocean.

I had a good idea where he was going now. I made the turn and got him back in sight just as he pulled up to the curb at the Beautiful Beach Real Estate office. As I drove slowly by, Lenny Conklin hopped out of his car and ran as fast as a fat man could into the building.

I kept going. No need to stop. I'd seen all I was going to see here — Lenny Conklin hurrying in for a visit with Ted Norris. A visit that obviously was instigated by my little chat with Conklin.

On the ride back to my cottage I tossed a few ideas around my confused brain, but couldn't come up with a good reason for Conklin's trip to see Ted Norris.

Chapter 34

I WAS HEADED HOME and had just turned down my street when I noticed a big black tank coming toward me from the other direction. There was something familiar about the car and I slowed a bit as we passed. All I could see was a large man driving. He was alone, or so I thought, until a blonde head suddenly popped up in the passenger seat and the driver reached over and forced it down.

Kelsey.

I jammed on the brakes and pulled a U-turn. My mouth went dry when I had to back up once to complete the turn.

I caught up to the car on O Street and followed it onto Ashworth. I wasn't sure what I was going to do, but I had to get Kelsey out of that car one way or the other. Right now the car was heading for the bridge. Lucky for Kelsey the bridge was in the open position. The car went as far onto the bridge as it could before stopping. I pulled to a stop and weighed my options. I didn't think the driver had spotted me.

A large party boat passed through the opened span. The bridge would close any second. If I was going to do something, I had to do it now, here in Hampton, before I got in a neighborhood I didn't know where I might lose them.

I jumped out of my car, fumbling for the .38 still at the small of my back. My heart thudded loud in my ears and my hands shook but I didn't have time to think about it. I dashed up to the driver's side door, the revolver held in both hands. The window of the car was down. "Get outta the car. Get outta the car, now."

The man behind the wheel was a big bastard with a mashed up face. His eyes looked familiar and when I heard him yell, "Fuck you," I recognized the voice. It was the big prick who'd beaten me senseless — Bozo the Clown. He could have been the one who killed Cora too. If so, he'd probably kill the boy — if I let him get away. I could see Kelsey beside him, a look of pure terror on the boy's face, the goon holding onto his T-shirt with his right fist.

Bozo stomped on the gas and I held my fire; Kelsey could've been hit. The black car plowed right through the gate that kept the traffic stopped, sending chunks of wood flying in all directions. I ran to my car, hopped in. The bridge began to close, but the operator, perhaps seeing what was going on, had suspended the bridge short of full closure. There was no way that Bozo could get across. And there was a forty-foot drop to the water below.

The black car slid sideways a few feet short of the bridge upright, engine racing. The passenger door flew open and Kelsey scrambled from the car. He ran to the side of the bridge and climbed up on the railing. I could see, even at this distance, the fear on his face. The boy had nowhere to go but over the side and into the water below. He glanced at my car.

He'd never make it. Not a chance.

The goon revved his engine. Was the maniac going to knock Kelsey off the railing?

Kelsey leapt back down and made a dash for my car. The black car sprang forward.

Kelsey wasn't going to make it.

I slammed into drive and floored the gas. My car fishtailed and burned rubber and for an instant I could see Kelsey out of the corner of my eye as I roared past and slammed hard into the driver's side of the black car. The goon bounced around in the front seat. He turned, stunned, glazed eyes looking toward me. The entire driver's door was pushed in and the glass had caved.

For a second, I just sat there trying to decide what to do next. The goon shook his head like a wet dog, drops of blood flying off. His right hand came up. He was holding a pistol. I put the car in reverse, went back about twenty feet. The few cars that'd been behind me had backed off the bridge. I dropped into drive, and hit the gas hard once more, holding on to the wheel for dear life and aiming directly for the goon pointing his big gun at me. Just before I reached him, I heard an explosion and my windshield spiderwebbed. Seconds later the world exploded again as I slammed into the side of the black car. My head snapped forward and my vision blurred.

I couldn't see the goon and for a minute I thought he might be dead. But his head lifted back into view, then his arm. The bastard still had the gun in his hand. The same bastard who'd almost beat me to death, had probably hurt Dianne and Shamrock, and maybe killed Cora. If I didn't end this now, he'd keep after Kelsey until he killed the boy, too. I nailed the gas pedal and my car started pushing his up the little incline, inches at a time. I backed off a bit and slammed into him again, pushing him a couple of more feet. I kept the gas pedal down, moving his car in little spasms. The goon was trying to get a shot off but his arm didn't seem to be working right. The jerky movements of his car didn't help him get a bead on me either.

Suddenly, his car sagged away from me a bit and a look of animal fear crossed his jailhouse face. I stomped on the gas once more and the black car upended, disappearing over the open edge. I heard a violent crash as the car hit the other side of the span, and then moments later, a splash as the car hit the water far below.

I jumped out of the car and Kelsey raced toward me. He ran right into my arms and we held onto each other. He was crying and I could feel his body shaking; maybe mine was too, I wasn't sure. People were shouting and running up to us, but I didn't care what they were saying. Some were peering down over the open chasm where the black car had ended up. And somewhere off in the distance I could hear sirens. Lots of sirens.

I had a quick mental debate with myself—did I want Kelsey here when the police arrived? There was a better-than-even chance that if the cops got their hands on the boy, he'd eventually be turned over to his father, Ober Sweeney. I couldn't let that happen. On the other hand, if I ran from what I assumed might be a dead body under the Hampton Bridge, from an accident I had caused, I'd get picked up for sure. Under those circumstances it might be a little more difficult to extricate myself from any possible legal repercussions. I grabbed Kelsey's hand and towed him through the crowd, away from my wrecked car. A few people stared but no one tried to stop us. When we were off the bridge and jogging past the state park, I could still smell burning tire rubber and the odor of boiled radiator water. I slowed my pace, and Kelsey followed suit. Police cruisers, sirens wailing and lights flashing, flew down Ashworth zig-zagging around traffic that by now was backed up. I slowed our pace even further. A man and a boy running away from the action would be sure to attract a cop's attention. The police cars zoomed past us.

"Where are we going?" Kelsey asked. His face was flushed and his blue eyes watered.

I still held his hand tight. "The cottage."

When we rounded the corner of Eaton I broke into a trot, pulling Kelsey along with me. Between the cottages on my right I could see the bridge and all the hullaba-loo. Police cars were there now, lights still flashing, and it looked like Seabrook cruisers had come on the bridge from the opposite side. Ambulances also had joined the party. A few residents came out of their cottages and hus-tled past us in the opposite direction.

One tall skinny man with a mullet haircut and an "Iron Maiden" T-shirt tried to buttonhole me as we passed. "What the hell happened?" he asked.

"Someone jumped off the bridge," I gasped. "Landed on a party boat passing below."

"Jesus Christ!" He turned and broke into a dead run in the direction of the so-called tragedy.

By the time we reached the cottage, Kelsey and I were both gasping for breath. I couldn't smell anything from the wreck anymore and the air was clear this close to the ocean. Still, my lungs burned. On the porch, I fumbled with the keys, then noticed the door around the lock was splintered. The goon had probably busted in the door before Kelsey had even realized what was happening.

I pushed the door open. We stumbled inside and I slammed it behind us. The door didn't latch.

Kelsey looked terrified. Between gasps, he said, "What's...the matter? Why did...we run?"

Between longer gasps, I answered, "We...had...to."

"We didn't do anything wrong."

I grabbed Kelsey by the shoulders and guided him over to the sofa. I sat beside him, took a minute to regain my breath. "No, we didn't do anything wrong. But I think you're still in danger, Kelsey."

Kelsey forced a smile, looking for all the world like he was the adult and I was the child. "But that was the guy who chased me, Dan. We don't have to worry anymore. He must've killed Ma, too."

"I'm not so sure of that." I wiped sweat from my forehead and glanced at the unlatched door. "Look, we haven't got much time. What happened? What did he say to you?"

Kelsey didn't have the smile on his face anymore. "I was watching TV and he crashed through the door." He looked at me apprehensively. "I didn't have time to get in the attic."

"I know. Don't worry about that. What did he say?"

"Nothing, Dan. He dragged me into his car. He had a big gun." The boy's body shook. "He just told me to shut up. Then you came."

"Are you sure he didn't say anything?"

"Just, 'Shut up, shut up.'"

I didn't want to scare the boy any more than he already was but I had to tell him enough so he'd know we were still in danger. "I don't think he killed your mother, Kelsey. And if he did, he was just working for someone else. I don't know yet who that someone is but he's still out there. And until I can get the real killer off the streets, we have to be very careful. No one can know where you are. You understand?"

Kelsey nodded.

The sirens still screamed in the distance. By now tow trucks were probably on the scene and for a moment I let myself wonder how they'd get the black car and its big occupant out of the drink. Then I took a deep breath. The incident would be all over the papers tomorrow. I could catch up on the details then. If I wasn't behind bars.

"Good," I said, ruffling Kelsey's hair. "We haven't got much time. The cops'll be here soon. I want you up in that attic. Be quiet and don't come out for anyone but me."

He nodded vigorously. "Will you be okay? What will they do to you?"

I wasn't sure but he didn't need to know that. "I'll be fine. Like you said, we didn't do anything. They might take me for questioning but I'll get back here as soon as I can."

I led him into the kitchen and threw a gallon of water, some non-refrigerated yogurts, and a few bananas and apples along with a couple of skateboard magazines into a bag. I hurried him into the middle bedroom, pointed to the attic trap door. Kelsey scrambled up onto a hamper, pushed the trapdoor aside, and boosted himself into the attic. After he was up, I handed the bag of food to him. He looked down at me through the hole, his face a frightened mask.

"Close the door, Kelsey. And stay quiet."

He fit the trap door back in place. Just in time. I heard tires screech and car doors slam. I ran from the bedroom into the front room and stood for a moment, staring at the front door. Feet clomped up the porch steps. What had probably been intended as a loud knock sprung the unlatched door open. Two Hampton cops stood just outside the door.

The closest held his handgun by his side. "Dan Marlowe?" he said. I nodded. "Put your hands on your head."

I did. They both entered. The second cop spun me around and pulled my arms behind my back. He put handcuffs on me, cold steel pinching my skin. It had been a long time since I'd worn metal bracelets. They didn't feel any different.

One cop held my arm as we did the perp walk out and down the porch stairs to stand beside the cruiser. A few of my neighbors were out enjoying the excitement. I didn't mind too much. After all, I always enjoyed watching an arrest. Everybody on the beach did. This was just my turn. Within a few minutes the second cop came out of the cottage and yelled, "There's no one here."

I let out the breath I'd been holding as I climbed into the backseat of the police car.

Chapter 35

IT HAD BEEN a long time since I'd toured Ocean Boulevard handcuffed in the back seat of a police car. Knowing that they hadn't found Kelsey made the ride almost enjoyable. The cacophony of cackling mannequins and the aroma of brick-fired pizza filled the cruiser as we shot past the Casino. The tour didn't last long; the driver had the lights flashing and siren screaming like we were headed for a terrorist bombing. Drove that way too.

When we reached the one-story cinderblock police station out back on Ashworth, the driver whipped the cruiser into a reserved spot near the front door. Together the cops hauled me out of the back seat and I was offered another chance to perfect my perp walk. A young guy with a peach-fuzz beard and press tag snapped photos of me as I trudged along.

He jumped in step with me. "Mr. Marlowe. What happened? Did you kill someone?" His voice was shaking.

I figured he was with the *Hampton Union* and probably heard the excitement on his police scanner. I said the only thing that came to mind. "No comment."

The reporter looked crushed as we bulled through the front doors, leaving him standing outside looking in.

Inside I was hustled into a room marked "Interrogation." I didn't like that word. The cop who'd driven the cruiser entered the room with me, removed one of the cuffs, forced me to sit in a metal chair, and attached the free cuff to the arm of the chair. I shifted position and noticed the chair was bolted to the floor.

"Now what?" I asked.

"You gotta wait," the cop said as he backed against a blue tile wall, bumping into a pay phone as he did.

To pass the time I took a survey of the room. I was seated at a rectangular, brown conference-type table, covered by what looked like a spill-resistant material. There was one other chair at the opposite end of the table. Looked like that chair was floor-bolted too. The table was bare except for an ashtray in the middle with lobsters and the words "Greetings From Hampton Beach" printed on it. No butts were in the tray but it was smudged with ash. Over my shoulder I wasn't surprised to see a large wall mirror, probably two-way. Overhead were fluorescent lights attached to a false ceiling. In addition to the door we came in, there was another with "Exit" above it. A few file cabinets against another wall, with document boxes piled on top of them, and some type of camera hanging from the ceiling pointed at the table just about finished the inventory and the time I could waste with it.

Just then the door flew open and a hurricane breezed in. Of course I'd seen him around the beach and I knew the hurricane's name was Gant. I didn't know his rank. He didn't help any, rattling off his identification so fast I didn't catch any of it. Lieutenant or captain, judging by the way the cop against the wall came to ramrod attention. Gant wasn't in uniform, so no help there. He wore a sport coat and tie with dark pants that had a crease that looked sharp enough to cut your hand. His receding white hair was combed straight back. His face was thin and deeply lined, yet it looked like that of an exercise addict. His body looked the same. I pegged him as an ex-marine and wondered where he'd gotten his tan.

Gant plunked himself down in the chair opposite me and dropped a brown folder on the table. He opened the folder, put a pair of glasses on and let them hang on the tip of his nose. He peered over the glasses at me. "Daniel Marlowe."

I assumed that wasn't a question so I didn't say anything. We stared at each other.

Finally he lowered his eyes to the papers in front of him. "Nice history you got here, Mr. Marlowe." There was a sarcastic tone to the *Mister* part. "Let's review: Disorderly Conduct, Driving Under the Influence, Restraining Order Violation. Oh, here's an oldie but goodie—Possession of a Controlled Substance. You're a regular one-man crime wave."

"That was a while ago."

"Maybe it was. But what don't we know about?"

I raised my cuffed hand as far as I could. "Am I under arrest?"

Gant took his glasses off. "Not yet, but we've got a murder investigation going on here and you're our prime suspect."

"Murder? What murder?" Suddenly I had to fight to keep the anxiety under control.

Gant leaned a little closer. "We got a car with a body in it obstructing boat traffic under the bridge. Somebody rammed that car off the bridge. What would you call it?"

"It was self-defense."

"Self-defense? You shoved him over a bridge, car and all. I'm surprised you didn't poke his eyes out first."

"He shot at me."

"Maybe it was self-defense on his part."

"It wasn't."

"Then tell me what happened."

I figured I had nothing to lose, so I told him most of the story.

When I was done, he folded his arms across his chest, leaned back and stared at me with those hard blue eyes. "That's a nice tale, Marlowe. Fits with some other things we've been hearing about you lately. Most of which has not been good, by the way."

"I can't help what people say."

"Where there's smoke there's usually fire."

"You said I wasn't under arrest." I held the cuffed hand up again and shook it.

Gant turned to the cop still standing by the wall. "Take 'em off," he said. Then added, "You search him?" The cop looked sheepish. "Do it," Gant said.

The cop came over, ran his hands up and down my body, and then emptied my pockets. He tossed my wallet, keys, loose change, and of course my prescription bottle on the table.

Gant reached over, picked up the vial, and put his glasses back on to read the label. "This legitimate?" he asked.

"It's a doctor's prescription."

"A nervous Nellie, huh?"

I didn't like the way he said that, but the cop was removing the handcuff, so I kept my mouth shut. When the cuff came off, I rubbed the red mark around my wrist.

Gant pointed his index finger at my face. "If what you're saying is true...and you haven't sold me on it... you still might be a candidate for a manslaughter charge. I don't appreciate people being tossed off the bridge on my beach."

I raised my voice. "I told you, he was going to kill the boy. I had no choice."

"That's what you say. I haven't heard that particular story from anybody else yet."

"You can look at the damn bullet hole in my windshield. I didn't put the goddamn thing there myself."

Looked like Gant didn't like people arguing with him. "From what I've been hearing, you're lucky other people haven't been taking potshots at you. You been sticking your nose where it doesn't belong."

"Somebody's got to. Nobody else is doing the job."

Gant jumped up. For a second it looked like he was going to come at me. He slammed his hands down on the table and leaned in toward me. "Look, shithead. Everybody here is doing their job. You just don't know when to mind your own business." He poked his finger hard into my chest. "You keep your nose on your face where it belongs. We're taking care of things."

I was just about to say something I probably would've regretted when the door opened and Steve Moore walked in. He was dressed as usual and looked uncomfortable when he saw Gant poking at me.

"Could I speak to you a minute," Steve said, looking at Gant.

Gant pushed himself away from the table. Steve drew him over to the far corner and mumbled in a low voice. Gant's face turned dark and he looked at me as he listened. When Steve was done, Gant came back to the table and took his seat. Steve remained where he was.

"All right, Marlowe. It looks like some of what you said happened at the bridge might be true." Gant looked like he was admitting he believed in flying saucers. "But where's the Sweeney kid?"

I looked Gant directly in the eyes. "He disappeared in the crowd."

Gant looked at me for a long time. "I don't believe you."

"Why would I lie?"

Gant looked back at Steve. "I don't know, but I'm going to find out."

"Be my guest."

Gant played with the folder a bit. Then a smug look came over his face. "What I said about the manslaughter charge stands. It's still a possibility."

No one said anything for a minute. I wanted out of there. "Can I go?" I said.

Gant waved at my possessions on the table. "Yeah, take your stuff with you. And don't take any vacations. We'll be in touch."

I gathered up my change, wallet, keys, and just before I reached for my scrip, Gant said, "Don't forget your nerve pills." He had a little smirk on his face. I grabbed the prescription bottle and shoved it in my pocket.

On the way out of the room I glanced at Steve Moore. He looked away. I slammed the door behind me. Cops!

Chapter 36

STEVE MOORE AND I sat on my porch, both of us rocking aggressively. "Look, Steve, you can't take the boy," I said, almost pleading. "I know you wouldn't give him to his father, but someone else might, and judging by what's happened recently Kelsey could be dead before the next high tide."

Steve took a pull on his Heineken. "Not only can I take the boy, Dan, I have to. Gant said to get him and get him yesterday."

The night was crystal clear, the smell of salt water swept over the dunes and the air was perfectly quiet.

"Screw him."

"That's easy for you to you say. He's my boss and he's a hard ass."

"Gant doesn't know the danger the boy's in. You do." I stopped rocking and looked at Steve.

Steve stopped rocking and looked right back at me. "I can't be risking my job over this."

"Over what?" I scoffed. "Him?" I nodded toward the closed window behind us. Steve turned and looked in at the back of the blonde head watching television.

After what had transpired at the bridge Steve had figured I wouldn't let Kelsey out of my sight. And being a beach person he knew there weren't too many places you could hide a kid in a five-room cottage. So he called my bluff, showed up on my doorstep, and threatened to climb up into the attic. I'd told Kelsey to come on down. Now I had to convince Steve that taking the boy to Gant wasn't necessarily the best option.

"Child Services will take him and he'll be back with Sweeney the next day."

Steve let out a sigh and started rocking again. "We don't know if his father has anything to do with any of this."

"We don't know that he doesn't either. And it's not just him I'm worried about. That girlfriend of his, Mona Freeman. She's a piece of work. She threatened to have me taken care of. And that character down at the bridge? Ahh..."

"Ambrose. Clay Ambrose. Freelance muscle from Lowell."

"Yeah. And I wouldn't be surprised if he was sent by Sweeney or Freeman."

"To work you over and snatch his own kid. What for? Where's the payoff for that type of stuff? I think it's pretty farfetched."

"Not if Sweeney killed Cora and believes Kelsey saw him and that Kelsey told me. And what if it was Mona Freeman? If Kelsey gets turned over to his father, you're turning the boy over to her too."

Steve held up his empty green Heineken bottle, jiggled it. I got up, got us two more, and returned.

"All right," he said. "I agree with you that it wouldn't be safe to have the kid end up with his old man. Still, Gant wants to find him and told me to check your place again."

Looked like I was finally winning him over, whether it was my power of persuasion, or beer power, I didn't know or care. "You could say you did and he wasn't here. They'd believe that."

"Not for long. For Chrissake, Dan, this isn't some rinky-dink thing going on here. You killed someone. Granted, he was a sleazebag and had a record a mile long, but if there weren't witnesses that said he was trying to snatch the kid, you'd be sitting in jail right now charged with manslaughter. You still might be. When I left the station, the chief, Gant, and a couple of state cops were going over the whole mess. They're checking out your line of thinking now — trying to tie Cora Sweeney's murder to the action at the Tide, your beating, the kid's kidnapping, the whole ball of wax. They're going to see if they missed something the first time around."

I tried, unsuccessfully, to keep the sarcasm out of my voice. "You mean they think they might've missed something?"

Steve got defensive. "Okay, okay. So maybe you were onto something. You gotta remember, we run into people dying all the time and most deaths are either natural, accidental, or self-inflicted, nothing more. So we have a right to be skeptical when something looks like a natural death and somebody..." He gave me a pissed-off look. "...like you, for instance, comes up and shouts murder without one sliver of evidence to back it up."

"What if you stalled Gant and the rest of them for a few days? Tell him the boy took off or something. Tell him you're sure you could locate him within that time. Could you do that?"

Steve took a long sip of beer and looked up at the stars before answering. "Probably. I guess. But what good would a few days do? You still don't know who's behind all this. And even if you did, how are you going to prove it?"

"Maybe by making an offer the killer can't refuse."

"The killer's dead, Dan. You pushed him off the goddamn bridge. Remember?"

I smiled. "I'm thinking he was just a hired hand. Freelance muscle you called it. So who hired him—Ober Sweeney, Mona Freeman, Lenny Conklin, Ted Norris or Frankie Quail? Or some combination thereof?"

Steve glared at me, fire in his eyes. "So what are you gonna do...tell half the beach the kid's here and see who shows up to whack him?"

He had part of it right but not the important part.

"I wouldn't do anything that could hurt that boy." I looked over my shoulder, saw the back of Kelsey's head through the window, the glare of the TV. "He's not going to be here."

"So what if another muscle-head shows up? Where's that leave you? You still wouldn't know who's behind this mess."

"I think the main man would come himself this time. Ronald Reagan'll hear about his buddy's demise and make himself scarce. I don't think whoever's behind this would want to risk any other lowlifes knowing what he's done. Whoever it is, I'm betting he or she will try to take care of it without calling in anyone else who could put the finger on him later. If he's got any brains, that's how he'll handle it."

"Some criminals don't have any brains, Dan."

"I got a feeling this one does. So what do you say—can you give me three days?"

Steve studied his Heineken, swirling the beer round and round in the bottle. "I'd have to be involved in the whole thing. No going behind my back. I'd be putting my butt on the line."

"I understand. No problem. Matter of fact, I'll need your help."

"Hmm. I'll bet you will. But I'm going to wait until tomorrow to give you an answer. You got me half in the bag here, and I want to see if I still feel as generous when I wake up in the morning."

I laughed. "That's fair enough. You tell me in the morning, and if it's a go, we'll talk about how we're going to keep the boy alive and catch a killer."

"You put it that way, I'd have to have a real bad hangover to say no, wouldn't I?" He put the beer to his mouth and tipped it too quick. A stream fell down his chin onto his shirt.

"Yeah, you would." I made a half-hearted grab for his beer. "You're shut-off."

Steve laughed. "Like hell I am." He held up the empty beer, shook it. "Come on, bartender. You wanna shtay on my good side, more beer."

When I went in to get the beers, Kelsey was asleep on the couch, the glow from the TV the only light in the room. After what he'd been through today, I didn't dare wake him. I'd been worried he'd never be able to sleep again. I covered him with a blanket and put a pillow under his head. He looked so peaceful. Hard to believe someone would do almost anything to see him dead.

Chapter 37

WHEN I CRAWLED out of bed the next morning, I thought I could hear the waves slamming against the jetty. It took me a moment to realize it was just the pounding of my head. Before I'd gone to bed the night before, I'd moved Kelsey into his bedroom; he was still out cold. I waited until I'd finished my first cup of coffee, then called Steve. He had a king-size hangover too. No surprise considering all the beer I'd pumped into him. What was a pleasant surprise though, was that he still grudgingly agreed to go along with my plan. He'd stall Gant for three days. Not only that, he volunteered to let the boy stay with him. Said he'd pick him up tomorrow morning. We'd both known that Kelsey couldn't stay here with me, not with what I was planning. The fact that he'd be with Steve while I tried to get myself killed eased my mind a lot. He had one other request—I had to swear never to tell anyone about his involvement. I agreed.

Our plan was simple but not original. We were going to let our suspects know that Kelsey was staying with me and that within a few days he was going to be brought before a grand jury looking into Cora's death. Steve was going to pay Frankie Quail a visit. His lawyer had gotten him out on high bail and he was back at his T-shirt shop. So Steve was going to drop in, pretend to harass him, and drop the grand jury info into the harangue. He was also going to make a phone call to Ober Sweeney, informing the man that he could have custody of his son after the grand jury testimony. That would take care of Mona Freeman too. I was left with Lenny Conklin and Ted Norris. Since I'd trailed Conklin to Beautiful Beach Real Estate, I figured tipping off one of them would get the dope to the other one, too. I chose to approach Ted Norris. I was less likely to lose my cool with him than with Conklin.

Before I left the cottage, I had two things to do. First, I called in a favor and got a co-worker to take my shift for the day. Second, I called Shamrock. He agreed to come, cane and all, and stay with Kelsey while I was gone. Sit shotgun, literally, with Betsy.

After Shamrock arrived, about eleven o'clock, I drove to the real estate office and found a parking spot right out front. Inside I ran into the same female receptionist as last time. She tried to stop me from going into Norris's office. I waved her off, opened the door, and walked right in.

Norris sat behind his desk. He looked up from a bunch of papers spread out in front of him. Every one of the man's white hairs seemed to be in the exact spot it had been in last time I'd seen him. Apparently he had a wardrobe of gaudy sport coats because he was wearing a different one today.

He looked like he wanted to chew me out for coming in without knocking but his sales training prevented it. "Mr. Marlowe, what can I do for you?"

I took a seat in front of his desk. "To tell you the truth, I was wondering if the Sweeney lot on Reed Street was available for sale? I've got some Massachusetts friends who are interested."

Norris cleared his throat. "I've got quite a few nice cottages and a couple of other lots on the beach that they might like."

I shook my head. "No, I've told them about that one and that's what they're interested in. They like the location."

Norris looked down and played with the papers in front of him. "Well, unfortunately, it's not for sale right now."

"When will it be?"

"I don't know."

"They'll pay top dollar."

"I'm sure many people will for that lot."

"In that area?"

The man's shoulders went up and I could actually see him bristle. "There aren't many vacant lots on the beach, Mr. Marlowe. And the area is improving."

"It couldn't do anything but," I tossed in.

"Would your friends like to look at anything else?"

"I'll ask them." I wanted to end this charade and was trying to figure out a way to broach the subject I'd come to talk about, when Norris bailed me out.

He shuffled some papers and tried to look a little too nonchalant. "Anything new on Mrs. Sweeney's death?" he asked, adding quickly, "I remember last time you were here you thought there was something more than suicide to it."

He watched me closely.

"Funny you ask. There is more to it, a lot more. As a matter of fact, a grand jury is looking into her death, along with some other incidents that've happened recently on the beach."

Norris's eyes widened. "Ohh? I did heard about your unfortunate incident down at the bridge. Someone was trying to harm the Sweeney boy?"

He'd bailed me out again. "Yeah. But he's ok. He's staying with me now. Monday he's scheduled to go before the grand jury." I heard the pen in Norris's hand click twice. "It should be all over then. He's been through a lot for a young kid."

"I'll say. It's a real tragedy." Norris played again with the papers on his desk. "Well, if there's anything I can do, I'd be glad to help out."

"No. Thank you, though." I stood and he stuck out his hand. I shook hands, trying not to grimace. His hand was like the rest of him — soft and pudgy and clammy. Not a good hand. Not a good man.

Chapter 38

THE PHONE STARTED RINGING when I stepped into the cottage. I grabbed the receiver on the second ring.

It was Steve Moore. "Dan, can you come down to the harbor?"

"What's the problem?"

"Why don't you just come down and see."

I turned to Shamrock who was seated on the couch with Kelsey. "Mind staying a bit longer?"

They were both engrossed in some super hero show I was unfamiliar with. Shamrock didn't take his eyes off the television. "Fine, Danny, fine."

"I'll be right down," I said into the phone.

I walked to the harbor in about five minutes. I didn't have any trouble finding Steve. He was standing by the shoreline surrounded by three police cars, a fire engine, rescue truck, town personnel, and assorted lookers-on. I wove my way through the crowd and stopped next to him. He stood, feet planted in the wet sand, looking down at a bloated body. The body resembled a small beached whale and had a similar odor. It also looked like the body of a forty-something male with bushy black hair, loud Hawaiian shirt, and a thick gold chain around the neck. I didn't even need to see the bandaged right hand to know who it was. A peanut of a man who I assumed to be a medical examiner, knelt beside the body, poking and prodding at the swollen carcass.

"Look familiar?" Steve asked without looking up.

"It's him," I answered. "Ronald Reagan. The guy who attacked Guillermo and Dianne in the kitchen and kidnapped me. I'm as sure as I can be without having seen his face before. Same shirt, same chain, same burnt hand. Even the hair on his chest is the same."

I watched as the medical examiner turned the victim's head to the side. There was a small round entry wound. "A .22?" I asked.

Steve nodded. "They go in but don't have enough strength to come out the other side of the skull. Instead, they just bounce around inside, making Swiss cheese of the brain. They're quiet too."

The day was already gray and the body laying in front of me didn't make it feel any brighter. The sight of the twin domes of the nuclear power plant across the harbor didn't do anything for my mood either. "Did you find him here?"

"One of the party boats found him. Whether he was killed here or washed up from somewhere else, we don't know yet. Probably doesn't matter, does it?" Steve tilted his head. "Let's take a walk."

He pushed through the crowd behind us and I followed. We walked farther out along the harbor and down a dirt road, passing rows of stacked boats.

"You know what this means, Dan?"

"I've got a good idea. What's his name?"

"It doesn't matter what his name is. We'll find that out soon enough." Steve slipped his mirrored shades off, wiped a smudge off a lens, crinkled his bloodshot eyes. He put the sunglasses back on crookedly. "What does matter is that you and I both know that he was the other guy who worked you over. And now he's dead, most likely killed by whoever the hell is behind all this. There's no one left who can put the finger on the killer. Except the kid, or so he probably thinks. And we've told everyone that the kid is staying with you. You told Lenny Quarters and Ted Norris, right?"

I nodded. "Yeah, I told Norris and I know he's tied in with Conklin so I'm sure he'll get the message too."

Steve turned toward me and we stopped walking. "For once I wish I hadn't been so quick to agree," Steve said. "Unfortunately, I've already told both Sweeney and Quail too. About the kid staying with you and that grand jury bullshit. I don't know how the hell I let you talk me into it."

"Lots of beer."

"This is serious, Dan. I think we should call this whole thing off. Let me give you and the kid some protection for a while. We can nail this guy some other way."

We walked in silence right up to the edge of the docks, then turned and walked back the way we'd come.

"We knew this was dangerous when we decided to try it," I finally said. "Finding another dead body just makes it all the more important that we go through with what we've started. Kelsey's the only one left to get rid of. The only one left who they think can connect the killer to Cora's death. Whoever he is, or she for that matter, he's gotten himself in deep and now he'll kill anyone if it'll help dig him out."

Steve kicked at some pebbles as we walked along. "I don't like it. This character knows all about you; you know nothing about him. He can come for you at the cottage whenever he wants. If I thought there was another way..."

"There isn't. But maybe there's still a way to find out who we're dealing with beforehand. That might give us a little advantage." I'd had an idea rattling around in my brain for a while now that had been troubling me. "Have you heard anything about the property down near Cora Sweeney's? Any plans for the area or anything?"

Steve gave me a quizzical look. "No, why?"

"I don't know. I'm just wondering if there's something we're missing. With all that's happened, it's hard to believe there wouldn't be some larger motive behind it all."

"You'd be surprised what people kill for. If you look at some people the wrong way, they'll blow your brains out."

"I suppose so." I hesitated for a moment, then said, "Who knows most of what's going on around the beach? Things the average person wouldn't know? The Chamber of Commerce guy?"

"A bartender asking that question? You're kidding, right?" When he saw I wasn't, Steve continued. "The Chamber guy knows plenty but so do you bartenders. The only person that probably knows more is the mayor. She knows when someone blows their nose on the beach."

It didn't dawn on me right away who he was referring to, so I asked, "What mayor? We got selectmen."

Steve shook his head. "No, no, no. The mayor of Hampton Beach. You know—Seagull Sally."

Seagull Sally? "I never heard her called the mayor."

Steve chuckled. "It's a cop name. When we're in the cruiser and we see her, that's how we all refer to her: There's the mayor."

"So you actually think she picks up that much scuttlebutt?"

"You better believe it. She's out there all year, isn't she? She doesn't just have a big bag of bird food. She has big ears too. Doesn't miss a trick, that one."

"I never realized that."

We'd returned to the edge of the crowd and stopped walking. Steve turned to face me. "What the hell are you looking for, Dan?"

"I'm not sure." And I wasn't. "But with a little luck, Seagull Sally's seen more than just seagulls and pigeons."

Steve lifted his shades and peered at me. "I've got no idea what you're talking about, but be careful, will ya? We've opened a big can of worms here. You gonna stick around?"

"No. I'm taking off. Need to figure out how I'm going to find the mayor."

"Don't sweat it, the woman doesn't take a vacation. She feeds those birds 365 days a year. It's her calling or something." Steve dropped his shades back over his eyes, turned, and shoved his way through the crowd toward the decaying body.

I went the other way. It was afternoon—too late to look for Seagull Sally. She fed her flock earlier in the day; everyone knew that. I'd have to catch her tomorrow and hope she had more upstairs than her birdbrained friends.

Chapter 39

FRIDAY MORNING Steve came early and took Kelsey back to his place. I'd told Dianne I needed another day off. She hadn't complained; I was already scheduled to have Friday and Sunday off, so I just needed Saturday. Besides, she had an inkling of what I was up to and wanted to help. Even though we'd spread the word about Kelsey staying with me and his fictitious grand jury testimony on Monday, I still felt I had to speed things along. If the person responsible for Cora Sweeney's murder didn't make a move, then the boy's future wouldn't be bright.

It was about 10 a.m. when I hotfooted it up Ocean Boulevard. The weather was on my side—bright blue sky, about 75 degrees. I kept to the ocean side and hadn't gone far before I spotted a woman up ahead on the boardwalk just short of the playground. A large flock of seagulls and pigeons circled overhead like vultures. I walked faster, watching the woman take hunks of bread from a bag in her hand and scatter them about. The birds swooped and dived and fought among themselves for the handouts.

I reached her side and stood a few feet away. The birds took no notice of me. Usually seagulls and pigeons will fly off, at least a bit, when approached by humans. But with Seagull Sally there the birds apparently felt comfortable enough to tolerate other humans.

I didn't know the woman's name. I'd always thought of her as Hampton Beach's Seagull Sally. "Boy, they really seem to like you," I said, feeling foolish.

Seagull Sally was a tall, thin woman and when she turned to look at me I could see that one of her gray eyes was pointing off in a weird direction. "They damn well should," she said. "I feed 'em every day."

"What do you feed them?" I watched as a plump seagull came fluttering down to land on her duck-billed baseball cap. Except for her head bobbing with the weight, she paid no mind to the bird. I forced myself to look at her face and not the bird on her head.

"Anything. They eat anything. They're like a garbage disposal. I get stuff outta the rubbish, all sorts a stuff, mix it with old bread. They'll eat any damn thing and they love me for it."

"I can see that," I said. She'd stopped throwing the contents of her bag to the birds. Apparently they didn't like that because a few of them started barking loudly.

To my astonishment she suddenly began mimicking them. Her neck craned out and her neck muscles flexed.

She suddenly stopped and peered at me with her good eye. "I can talk to them you know. They understand me good. And they recognize me anywhere too. Once I went out to the Isle of Shoals on the day excursion. Second I got off that damn boat, wouldn't ya know, one a my birds recognizes me and comes flapping over, talkin' up a storm."

I forgot my mission for a second. "What did he say?"

Without missing a beat she let out a series of perfect imitations of a seagull's call. The woman wasn't joking; her face was as straight as a surfboard. I had trouble keeping mine as straight, but with effort, I did.

Seagull Sally began tossing food around again. The birds quieted right down, except when two decided to peck away at each other over a contested piece of eats. The bird on Sally's head suddenly sprang off and joined the feeding frenzy on the ground. Seagull Sally twisted her neck as if supporting the bird had given her a kink. Now was as good a time as any to get down to business.

"You've been coming here a lot of years, huh?" I asked.

"Longer than I can remember." She tapped her head with her index finger.

I hoped that had nothing to do with her mental condition. "So have I. Been an awful lot of changes through the years, don't you think?"

She stared at me with that lazy eye of hers. It was very distracting. "That's for sure. Not as many birds anymore."

"But a lot more buildings and people."

A mother, hand and hand with her little boy, strolled past us. The boy pointed and squealed at the sight of Seagull Sally and her feathered friends. The mother nodded and smiled, looking a little intimidated by the huge throng of birds. Or maybe she was leery of Sally herself. She tugged on the boy's arm and he reluctantly moved along, staring back wide-eyed at the birds as he left.

"Too many buildings," Seagull Sally said. "Too many damn people. And they ain't nice like birds. They cause trouble."

Time to steer the conversation in the direction I wanted. "And all the building...that's what's ruined the beach."

She slapped at the air. "Ahh. We ain't seen the worst of it yet."

Looked like I had her. "So you heard of something new coming? Maybe down around the Reed Street area?"

Seagull Sally held her arm straight out and one of the gulls flew up off the sidewalk, landing on her forearm. She peered at the creature from all sides, giving him a thorough inspection, looking for what I didn't want to know. "Somethin' new? I ain't heard of nothin' new coming to Speed City."

That derailed my train of thought. "Speed City? What do you mean, Speed City?"

She proudly adjusted her shoulders and the bird flew off her arm. "That's what I call the beach. Speed City."

I didn't know what Speed City had to do with anything but I was stuck with it. "Why Speed City?"

She flicked her thumb rapidly across her nose several times. "Ain't ya got a beak? Can't ya smell when they're cookin' that stuff? I can. It's mostly in the off-season though."

This was a million miles from where I'd figured our talk would go. "So you think someone's making speed on the beach?" Steve Moore had mentioned Ober Sweeney in regards to that, but nothing of any size to justify renaming the entire beach.

Sally cocked her head and gazed at me. Christ, the woman even looked like a bird. "I thought you was a bartender?" She pointed vaguely in the direction of the High Tide. "You're supposed to know everything." She gave me a sly grin. "Oh, yeah. I know who you is. There ain't a thing on the beach I don't know."

"So who's making all this speed?"

She slapped her forehead. "I ain't stupid. I ain't sayin'. Wouldn't even if I knew. And I don't know. I do know that I smell it at all different places on the beach, at different times."

Time to get back on track. "So you haven't heard of any building projects or developments trying to get going on Ashworth near Reed?"

She looked at me as if I was stupid. "Building projects? What's that? Nobody'd wanna build anything unless they wanted to lose money. You can't give condos away for free nowadays." She shook her head sadly, held up her hand, and rapidly rubbed her forefinger and thumb together. "Nobody's makin' money in real estate. It's the other stuff." Her thumb and finger moved so fast now I thought they might spark.

Her fingers didn't spark, but something suddenly sparked in my mind. Follow the money. How could I have been so dumb? The answer was right in front of me all along and I hadn't been able to see it. At least not until a woman with a bird on her head pointed it out to me. What was that saying about genius being close to madness?

It was the speed. A big operation not some little kitchen-sink setup. That had to be it. Big drugs equaled big money. And big money equaled a big motive for big crimes. It would explain a lot. Still, I wasn't convinced Ober Sweeney could run a large drug business like Seagull Sally had me envisioning.

Seagull Sally rattled on some more about the deterioration of the beach, but I'd already gotten all the useful information from her I was going to get. I spoke with her a while longer, then said good-bye. She wasn't rude but she didn't seem sad to see me go. She was more interested in her birds and they in her. As I walked away I looked back over my shoulder. She was doing her scarecrow impersonation—a bird perched on each of her outstretched arms and another plunked right on top of her noggin. I had a smile on my face the entire walk back to my cottage.

Chapter 40

SUNDAY NIGHT and I was still waiting for something to happen. Tomorrow Steve would have to tell the chief, or Gant, where Kelsey was hiding. I was wound up tight, sitting on my porch, rocking nervously and drinking Heineken when I heard someone come around the side of my cottage. He must have been crouching low, trying to stay out of my sight, because if he'd been upright I would've easily seen his head. Within seconds I could hear shoes on the porch steps and I stopped rocking. My throat went dry and my heart hammered hard in my chest. He took the three steps slowly and when his head popped up into view only a foot from mine, I wasn't shocked to see who it was — white-haired Ted Norris.

But he looked shocked to see me; he must've expected me to be protecting Kelsey, in the house with the door barricaded, not rocking away on my porch, sipping beer like I didn't have a care in the world. His eyes bulged and he started to say something, then shut his mouth and took the last step up to the porch. He had a gun in his hand, pointed at my head. I couldn't tell what kind it was in the semi-dark. The only light was the flickering glow from the television inside.

"Just sit there nice and easy, Marlowe," Norris said. "I want the kid and I want him now."

He seemed pretty calm, almost cocky, just like you'd expect from a successful real estate agent.

"He isn't here, Norris."

"Bullshit. Get up, we're going inside." He waved the gun. I stood up and he followed me into the cottage, flipped on the light, then jerked his chin at the couch. I quickly took a seat at the end beside the phone. He stayed standing, looking around.

"Okay, where is he?"

"I told you he isn't here."

"You better hope he is if you want to live."

I knew that was a lie; there was no way he could kill Kelsey and let me live. Norris waved the gun around, a long-barreled .22, the same kind he'd probably used to kill the thug down at the harbor. A nice quiet gun. An assassin's gun.

He took a step, still holding the pistol on me, and pushed open the door to my bedroom. He glanced into the room, checking it out. Then he moved to the kitchen doorway, looking into the kitchen and back again. He was about to move toward the other bedrooms when a ceiling panel crashed down on the living room floor. Both Norris and I looked up. I was just as surprised as he was. A sneakered foot protruded from the hole where the fallen panel had been.

"Not here, huh?" Norris said. He shot me a disdainful look. "Come on. Get the hell down here. Now."

The foot disappeared back up into the attic. "You got three seconds to get down here, kid," he shouted. He waited ten. Then he looked at me and smiled. Norris raised his gun and fired a shot about six inches to one side of the hole in the ceiling. Then he quickly let off another round about six inches to the other side of the hole. "You hit, kid?" Norris said a sneer on his face.

I made a move, but he swung the pistol in my direction. "You want to make it a little sooner, Marlowe, then come on."

He pointed the pistol at the ceiling again. I was sure he'd empty the gun if necessary.

"Kelsey, come down here." My original plan was out the window. I just hoped I could buy us a little time.

Norris drew the pistol back and within a few seconds I could hear movement above us and then in the middle bedroom as Kelsey apparently dropped through the trap door. Norris kept an eye on me as he walked to the bedroom, leaned in and yanked Kelsey out, pushing and shoving the boy into the room toward me.

When he saw me, Kelsey blushed and looked toward the floor like he thought I'd be mad at him for coming here and not staying put at Steve Moore's like he'd been told to. He was right, I was mad. But not at him. Norris had both of us together now. There was nothing stopping him from getting rid of us.

Kelsey stood there, skateboard in hand. "I'm sorry. I snuck out. Came in when you were in the bathroom. I wanted to help you."

"It's all right," I said. "Forget it."

He looked up at me, doubt written on his face. I didn't think he realized what serious trouble we were in.

"Put that stupid thing down," Norris said. Kelsey leaned the skateboard against the sofa near me. "You caused me lot of worry, kid. You and that crazy drunk mother of yours."

"She wasn't a drunk," Kelsey said, his small fists balling.

"And she wasn't crazy either, Norris." I had to keep him talking until I could come up with something. "She probably knew what you were up to. You didn't want her out of that cottage so you could make a few extra grand on summer rents. And there wasn't any new development planned for that area. You wanted that place for one of your meth labs."

Norris sneered. "So you figured that out, did you? Well, you're partly right, genius. I didn't need that dump to have my man do his cooking. I had the perfect setup for that—the cottages I handle the rentals on. A lot of the owners shut 'em down in the off-season. Of course, being their rental agent, I got the keys. And nobody gets suspicious noticing a well-known beach rental agent around a property, especially seeing my rental sign's hanging on most of them. I also know which owners are in places like Florida for the winter and when they'll be back. Do you think anybody thought anything when my man was there? Why would they? All they'd see is a loaded-down contractor's truck in the driveway and the rental agent visiting every so often, to see how his work's going. Not bad, huh?"

I had to keep him talking. "Yeah, pretty sweet. But I still don't understand why you had to..." I glanced at Kelsey. "... you know."

Norris poked the gun at me. "You aren't that dumb, Marlowe. You must know who my cook was by now." He nodded toward Kelsey. "I told him not to get that bitch riled up. She knew about our operation from when the two of them were together. Would he listen to me? No. Doing too much of my product. The stupid bastard was ripping her off for peanuts. And I was paying him damn well. You know what they say about a woman scorned, Marlowe. She threatened to go to the cops, spill our business to them. I couldn't let that happen."

"So you had to..." I glanced at Kelsey. He was just standing there, looking at Norris. I wasn't sure how much he understood.

"That's right...I had to," Norris said. "I didn't want to. I offered the crippled bitch money, but she wouldn't take it. She had to be either stupid or crazy."

"She wasn't either," I shot back. "The little I know about you, Norris, is that what you consider good money was probably nickels and dimes. Especially to a woman in a wheelchair. Even if she had agreed to your bribe, it probably would have been to get herself and her son off the beach, away from you and to safety. Instead of coming up with an offer that'd help her do that, you got greedy. Decided to keep the dough in your own pocket and get rid of the threat. That's when you came up with the idea of getting her drunk and pumping her full of pills."

Kelsey whimpered. He was staring at me as if I was killing his mother all over again. Felt like I was, but I had to stall for time. Whether it would do us any good or not, I didn't know. But as long as we were talking, Norris wasn't shooting and Kelsey and I were still alive.

Norris let out a wicked snicker and for the first time I noticed that his white hair in the light of the lamp bulbs looked yellow, same as his teeth. "Believe me, it wasn't hard getting her drunk. The pills weren't a problem either. I just crushed them up and sprinkled them in her booze every chance I got. I must've put twenty in the dumb broad's drinks." He let out a mean little laugh.

"But you didn't think it was so funny when she was finally dead and you heard the kid sneaking out the window," I said. "You figured he'd seen what you'd done to his mother. Nothing funny about that. Was there, Norris?"

Norris looked like he was going to shoot both of us right then, but instead he said, "The kid was supposed to be asleep. If it wasn't for him, it would've gone like I planned."

Now it was my turn to let out a mean little laugh. "It wasn't Kelsey that messed up your plans, Norris. It was you. The kid didn't see what you'd done to his mother. He snuck out every night of the week. Took his skateboard out the window and went flying around the beach. Every night, Norris. He didn't see a thing and didn't know who'd been with his mother."

Norris looked ashen for a minute, then slowly the color seeped back into his face. "Doesn't matter now," he said. "A lot of water's gone under the Hampton Bridge since then."

"Yeah," I said. "Like trying to kill the owner at the High Tide."

"You're off about that, Marlowe. I was trying to put you out of the picture. My man didn't do a good job. His timing was off. Tough getting good help nowadays."

I would've loved to wipe the grin off his face, but I looked at his gun and the distance between us and knew I'd never make it. "So you killed your strong-arm man because you figured punks like that'd give you up sooner or later. Or maybe you didn't want to pay him either."

Norris nodded. "Both. But I only had to take care of one of them. You did the other. Thanks for the favor." He let out another one of his sick little snickers.

"There's one thing I don't get, Norris—why did you blow up Cora Sweeney's place?"

Fire came into Norris's eyes. "Just before she passed out she told me she'd written something that'd hang me. I tried to get her to tell me where it was. But it was too late; she was gone."

"So when you couldn't find her little note, you figured her being in a wheelchair meant she only could've put the note somewhere close by. She couldn't go anywhere else. And that's why you weren't anxious to sell the lot either. You wanted to go through the goddamn rubble first. Make sure what you thought she'd hidden hadn't survived the explosion. I doubt there ever was anything written down. She got the last laugh on you, Norris."

"Maybe she got a laugh, but I'm having the last laugh." He jiggled the gun.

"And you think you're going to get away with all this?"

"Of course I am."

"The police know what I know. I've told Steve Moore everything."

Norris shrugged. "You were speculating. And besides, he's just a local yokel. He's not going to be able to prove a thing."

"And what will they think when they find...?" I started before catching myself.

Norris eyes narrowed. "You and the kid?" He pulled out a few magazines he had rolled up in his back pocket. He tossed them on the sofa beside me. I saw enough to know they were kiddie porn. "They'll figure you couldn't take the guilt anymore. Killed the kid, then yourself. With your reputation and your bum marriage, they'll swallow it."

My stomach lurched. Funny how some things can seem worse than death. "You've been quite an actor all these years, Norris. So I'm figuring those came from your personal stash." I spit at the magazines beside me.

Norris's face turned dark and angry. "Enough of this shit, tough guy. Let's see how brave you really are, Marlowe. I'll give you a choice: who dies first—you or the kid?"

I looked at Kelsey. He looked back, his eyes wide and scared. For a minute it was my own son standing there, silently pleading. My voice shook, "Him first. Him."

Norris sneered again. "That's what I figured, Marlowe. No wonder your wife left you. All right, I'll do the kid first. I like the idea of you watching. Pay you back a little extra for all the trouble you've caused me."

Norris slowly turned the gun from me to Kelsey. As he did I let my arm dangle over the side of the sofa until I found what I was looking for. I grabbed the skateboard tight and lunged. The instant I came up from the sofa, Norris saw me and swept the gun in my direction. I clutched the heavy wooden skateboard tight in both hands as I brought it up fast, slamming the board hard into the side of Norris's head. The gun went off and I felt a sharp pain in my bicep. Norris flew backwards, landing heavily on his ass on the floor. For a moment his eyes looked like no one was home.

Blood spurted from an ugly gash on the side of his head. He shook himself and started to raise the gun. I took two quick steps forward, skateboard held over my head with both hands. Norris got off a shot and the slug nicked my leg. Before he could fire again I brought the board down on the top of his skull with every ounce of strength I had. The board splintered in two with one half flying up and bouncing off the ceiling. It didn't matter. I wouldn't need to hit Norris again.

I turned. Kelsey stood there, shivering and shaking violently. I dropped the jagged piece of board I had in my hands, went over to him, and wrapped my arms around his shoulders. He wasn't the only one shaking.

"It's all over, Kelsey, it's all over," I kept saying. I finally stopped when Steve Moore knocked on the door.

Chapter 41

ABOUT A WEEK had passed since the Ted Norris incident down at my cottage. I'd gotten back to work as soon as the doctor said it was ok. The leg shot had only been a flesh wound. The bullet to my arm had missed the bone, but the wound was still heavily bandaged and sore as hell. I had to go slow building drinks but other than that, I was almost back to normal, whatever that was.

Hampton Beach was back to normal, too, it seemed. I figured with the death of Ted Norris that would be the end of the trouble on the beach, for a while at least. I should have known better.

"Dan, can I talk to you?" Dianne stood in the kitchen doorway. She looked the same as she always did for work—white spotted apron, hair tied back, a kitchen utensil in her hand. Not her face though; there were worry lines there I'd never seen before.

"Sure." I'd just stepped from behind the bar to let my relief take over the next shift. I assumed whatever she wanted to talk about had something to do with all that had gone on recently. I followed as she led the way through the bustling kitchen into her office. She sat behind her desk, the one that used to be mine, and I plopped down in the chair closest to her. It wasn't much of an office, but she kept it much neater than I had.

"What's up?" I suspected the answer wasn't going to be that my drink pour was too heavy. I was right.

Dianne let out a deep sigh. "I've got a problem. It's pretty serious."

"Anything I can do. You know that."

Dianne forced a little smile. "I hate to drag you into this after all you've been through. It's Crystal, my niece."

I didn't know Crystal. Not really. I'd seen her at the Tide once or twice visiting her aunt. Typical teenager. A pretty girl, even looked a bit like Dianne. I also knew that she was living with Dianne, had been for months now. What that was all about I didn't know and I hadn't asked. I waited for her to continue.

When she did, she got right to the point. "It's drugs. She's all screwed up, Dan. She's only fifteen and she's hanging out with some junkie who's got to be thirty."

I leaned forward, arms on my legs, cupped my hands. "What's his name?"

Dianne rubbed her hands together. "Oh, I don't know. Jingo, Jango, some stupid thing. Crystal thinks he's wonderful."

"Maybe it's his drugs she thinks are wonderful."

"Probably. Whatever it is I can't get her to stay away from him. I've tried everything but chaining her to her bed. Sometimes I don't see her for days, then she finally shows up all strung out on something. I don't know what."

"You've tried the cops?"

Dianne gave me an exasperated look. "Of course, I have. They've even brought her home a couple of times when I've called. But she goes right back to him within a couple of days."

"What about this Jingles guy?" I asked. "Can't they do anything about him?"

"It's Jango...or Jingo, oh now you've got me mixed up. I'd like to kill him."

"Why can't the cops take care of him?"

She shook her head. "No, no, no. They said the guy's not forcing her to go there and she tells them nothing happens."

"Go where? Where's this scumbag live?"

"The Honeymoon Hotel, room 210."

That didn't surprise me. The Honeymoon was a dump farther up Ocean Boulevard. Of course, that wasn't its real name, just what the locals called the place. It was a run-down firetrap that catered in the off-season to alcoholics, junkies, and people just down on their luck. During the summer the owner rented to kids of any age and looked the other way during their drunken bashes. Many times I'd seen teenagers hanging off the balconies, screaming drunk and waving their beer bottles, and wondered how none had managed to take a swan dive onto the pavement. Probably just a matter of time. The Honeymoon was always prominently featured in the *Hampton Union's* Police Log.

"What can I do, Dianne?"

She looked at me and I could see the tears welling. She was struggling to hold them back. I could hear the fear in her voice when she spoke. "I'm afraid if I don't get her away from him...she'll die."

She barely got the last two words out when the tears overflowed. I should have come around the desk and held her, but I didn't. Instead, I said lamely, "Dianne..."

She waved me off and reached for a small roll of paper towels on the desk. She ripped one off, wiping her eyes between sobs. I sat like a jerk, just looking at her. I probably felt as bad as she did. Finally her shoulders stopped heaving and she slowly regained her composure.

"I'm sorry, Dan," she managed to get out. "I just thought..."

This time I waved her off. I knew what she thought—that because I'd gone through the drug thing myself, maybe I had some magic wand that could save Crystal. I didn't have the heart to tell her that was a pipe dream. I couldn't even say I was completely reformed. I struggled every day. I still didn't know if I was going to win. How the hell could I ever get a teenager on the straight and narrow if I wasn't even sure about myself?

Still, I had to try to help. As long as the girl was alive, there was hope. But the longer she was with this Jingo character the less chance she'd stay alive. Besides, it was Dianne asking for the help. I owed her a lot. No matter what I'd recently been through.

"I'll see what I can do. I can't promise anything."

Dianne's face brightened. "I know. Thanks. Please be careful."

"Is this Jangles a tough guy?"

"It's Ji...oh never mind. I don't know anything about that. Just please be careful." Dianne got up from her chair, came around the desk, and headed for the door. I stood up and followed.

When she reached the door, she turned the knob and as the door opened inward, she stepped back—right into me. I stood flush against her. Her hair brushed my cheek. We both froze. She turned to look at me over her shoulder. That's when I gave up. I reached around her and gently closed the door. She secured the button lock. I slid my arms around her waist. She tilted her head, exposing the side of her neck, and I kissed her neck, slowly, along its length. She sighed. Neither of us said a word.

She turned toward me, looking up, eyes closed. She had a beautiful face. I liked everything about it, even the freckles across her nose. Our mouths were open before our lips touched. Our tongues played. I reached down, loosened the apron strings, let the apron fall away. I slowly undid the buttons on her blouse. She didn't wear a bra. Dianne pulled my shirt free from my pants, ran her hands up and under the fabric, across my stomach and chest.

I don't know whose hands were there first, but we were both fumbling with the snaps of the other's jeans. We only broke our kiss for a moment to pull everything out of our way. It was then that I got another look at that beautiful face smiling up at me. I was probably smiling too. I was so ready. It had been so long. So goddamn long.

Chapter 42

IT WAS AROUND noon time but you wouldn't have known it by the blanket of black clouds stretched across the sky. Felt like it could rain any second. Still, I felt good, even though I was apprehensive about what I was heading into. I was walking north on Ocean Boulevard. I'd promised Dianne yesterday that I'd do what I could about her niece and was on my way to keep that promise. The only way to handle the situation was to go right to the source of the trouble — The Honeymoon Hotel.

I was prepared; I had already popped a Xanax. The pill hadn't kicked in yet. My mouth was as dry as sandpaper. My palms were the opposite. I had considered bringing my revolver but decided against it. I had no idea what kind of person this Jango character was but I couldn't risk doing anything that would endanger

Crystal. If he was armed, I'd just have to come at the problem from another direction.

The streets weren't crowded. Fairly quiet too—just the sounds of occasional cars passing by and snatches of people's conversations. The fried dough stands were already pumping out their concoctions. The air was full of their sweet aromas.

When I got to the High Tide, a few twenty-somethings were just entering. I caught a look through the door before it swung closed. The place was jammed with the lunch crowd. I caught another look through the picture window as I passed. I didn't see Dianne. Still, I smiled.

I passed the two-block-long Casino building, trying to ignore the racket from the shooting gallery. Didn't want anything to interrupt my thoughts about what was going to happen in a few minutes, just a short distance up Ocean Boulevard.

When I reached the Honeymoon Hotel I stood on the sidewalk, hands on my hips, just checking it out. I don't know why I bothered. Maybe I was trying to build up my courage. The place certainly hadn't changed much since I'd first seen it. The bottom floor housed the standard T-shirt shop and an ice cream joint I knew handled the cheap stuff. Neither business was much to look at. A glass door separated the two. The glass was cracked from top to bottom. Above the ground floor were two floors of rooms for rent. The ones in front, facing the ocean, had balconies.

I rubbed my aching arm and tried not to think about the bullet I'd taken. I had pain killers but I hadn't thought it was wise to take one before coming here. I stared at the front door of the Honeymoon. My heart started to speed up and I began to feel that old familiar sense of dread rising up in me. I knew the feeling of doom had nothing to do with what lay ahead of me through the hotel door.

The symptoms fed on each other—fast heart, dry mouth, sweaty palms, foreboding—1, 2, 3, 4. The pill I'd taken earlier definitely wasn't working. Everything I'd been through the past few weeks was finally paying me a visit. I wanted to turn and walk away so bad. But where to? I couldn't walk away from this; if I did, the anxiety would march right along with me and this time it would never go away.

And then there was Dianne.

I took out the prescription bottle from my jean's pocket, removed another Xanax, tossed it under my tongue, let it dissolve. Then I took a deep breath, let it out slowly, and pushed through the front door.

I trudged up the skinny staircase heading for Room #210. The odor of Lysol stung my nostrils. The walls around me were peeling and the stairs were as rickety as they could be without collapsing. I wondered how the place ever passed a building inspection. It was the type of location no one would want to visit after dark.

I reached the second floor and found the room I was looking for. The number 2 was swinging loose from the door. My anxiety hadn't increased any — a good sign. In a moment I probably wouldn't have any time to think about my anxiety or anything else. That was a good thing too. I knocked forcefully.

"Yeah? Who's there?" came from the other side of the door. The voice was male and he sounded anxious too.

"Dan Marlowe."

"Get lost."

"Ok, but I'll be taking the fifty bucks I was going to give you for answering a few questions with me." The line wasn't original but I hoped it would get me through the front door.

"Questions? About what?"

"Crystal. Her aunt just wants to make sure she's all right. It'll mean fifty bucks for you." I could hear voices talking back and forth behind the door.

I stood there for a long minute. Finally, a deadbolt clicked and the door opened. I stepped inside. As I expected, it was your standard bottom-tier beach studio efficiency — a backbreaker of a double bed, a small sink with a hot plate on the tiny counter, three-foot-high fridge, and a Formica kitchen table with four mismatched plastic seat chairs. An ancient love seat and stained easy chair were the last of the furnishings. The one good feature was over on the far side of the room — floor-to-ceiling sliding glass doors that overlooked the Atlantic Ocean. Even from this distance, I could see that the balcony didn't look sturdy enough to hold more than a couple of drunken teenagers jumping up and down on it during the summer.

Two people were inside; they both looked like they belonged there. Mingled in with the smell of flat beer and cigarette smoke was a sickeningly-sweet body smell. I recognized it.

"Let's see the money, Pops."

When you're my age you can ignore that kind of name-calling and I did. The punk who'd tossed it at me was a junkie. And I didn't need Madam Marie, the beach psychic, to tell me that little bit of news. He stood near the balcony window, and if it had been open, a gust of wind could've sucked him out and bounced him along Ocean Boulevard. He didn't have enough meat on him to interest a mad dog. Other than that, the guy was average height with long black hair that looked like he'd forgotten how to wash it. He wore torn black jeans and a dirty, long-sleeved T-shirt with some heavy metal group logo on the front. His face was pock-marked and I guessed his age to be about thirty like Dianne had said. The man didn't seem able to stand still.

He held out an arm as thin as a broomstick and rubbed thumb and finger together rapidly. "The money. Where's the money?"

Over to my right, sitting on the sagging bed, was Crystal. I recognized her immediately even though she looked like she had deteriorated somewhat since the last time I'd seen her. Her clothes were in better shape than her boyfriend's, but she wasn't—she was as wired as he was. She looked her age—hell, she wasn't much older than my daughter—but I knew that wouldn't last long. She was still pretty, petite. I could see a resemblance to Dianne. The girl looked awfully scared and strung out. She bounced around the bed like the springs were jabbing her. I knew she could've used one of my pills, but that would have been a very temporary help. It was obvious what drug these two were doing. Meth. Apparently Ted Norris's demise hadn't done much good in cutting the drug's availability on the beach. From all appearances, they were probably both shooting it too. I'd seen it before.

I took out my wallet, removed a ten and two twenties. Jango took a step forward. "Not yet," I said. "I have some things I want to say first."

"Say 'em. Leave the money. Then get the hell out."

I turned to Crystal. "Your aunt wants you to come home."

"She don't wanna go home."

"I wasn't talking to you, Jango."

"It's Jingo, dude."

"That's what I said, Jingles." As long as this skinny scumbag didn't pull a knife or a gun, I'd have no trouble throwing him through the plate glass window behind him. I turned back to Crystal. "She's worried about you. She wants me to bring you home."

"Nobody's goin' home."

This guy must have been related to Ober Sweeney because his tics did the same kind of jitterbug across his face. "You let her answer, Jangles."

Crystal looked from the boyfriend to me, back and forth a few times. Like I said, she was strung out bad.

Finally, her blank gaze settled on her boyfriend. I knew she wasn't going to leave with me. I also knew the best thing for her would be a bust. But I could see why the cops would have a problem. Crystal and the punk were so juiced I was sure any dope the two of them got their hands on was up their arms and gone a minute after they got it, leaving no evidence behind.

I walked over to where Crystal sat on the bed and knelt down. She was a very pretty girl; I knew that wouldn't last long either. Her blue eyes were pinned. I touched her arm and she jerked. "Honey, I can take you out of here to your aunt. No one will stop us or hurt you."

I looked at the punk; he smirked. I turned back to the girl. "Come with me. It'll be all right." She was shaking and I suddenly realized she was so jacked-up she probably couldn't speak. I was familiar with all this. She wasn't leaving. Not right now.

When I stood, the punk grinned again. "I told you so. Now how about the money?"

"I want to use your can first, Jungo."

His tics quick-stepped. "This ain't a bus station."

"You sure of that?" I started for the only other door in the room. I was hoping he'd try to stop me. He didn't.

When I was inside the bathroom, I closed the door behind me. The room had a sink, toilet, shower stall. All filthy. I wouldn't have used the toilet if I'd had Montezuma's Revenge. I took out my prescription bottle of Xanax and dumped the contents in my hand. I put two pills back in the bottle and returned it to my pocket. A security blanket, but not for myself this time. If the girl did end up leaving with me, she'd need those pills badly. I took the rest of the pills, a couple dozen maybe, folded them up in some toilet paper, and stuck them under the bottom towel on a shelf. I didn't think the towels got much use.

I'd planned to try one more time to get Crystal to leave with me. But when I walked back into the main room, I could see that would be hopeless. The loser was beside her on the bed, his thin arm around her shoulders, stroking her hair and whispering to her. She was as stiff as a corpse, so paranoid she wouldn't walk out that door if God Almighty was holding her hand. So I didn't try.

As I walked across the room to the door, the punk said, "Hey, what about my money."

"I'll mail it to you, Jingle Bells." I couldn't in good conscious give them a dime. It would have been in their arms faster than a seagull on a stale piece of bread.

On my way back to my cottage I had time to think. And I could. The anxiety I'd felt earlier was gone. Whether the pills had finally kicked in or I'd simply forgotten to be anxious because of the confrontation at the Honeymoon or a combination of both, I didn't know or care. Instead, the anxiety had been replaced with a sense of resignation tinged with a touch of depression.

Depression because even after the death of Ted Norris and the collapse of his meth organization there still seemed to be plenty of dope to go around on Hampton Beach.

Resignation because I realized, and had probably always known, that the demise of one dirtbag like Norris would never change the big picture. There were probably a dozen like Ted Norris operating in the area. Smarter than Norris. Too smart to spoil a sweet setup like Norris had by killing someone like Cora Sweeney. That was the frightening part—that there were unknown others like Norris and that there always would be. There was nothing I or anyone else could ever do about it. There would always be someone to take their place.

There was something I could do about the situation with Crystal though and I was going to do it. I'd never ratted in my life. I didn't believe in spilling the beans on someone else. But Crystal wasn't much older than my own daughter. And again, Madam Marie wasn't going to make any money telling me how Crystal was going to end up. I didn't need her prediction—I already knew. I also knew it wouldn't take long to come true.

And then there was Dianne.

Any second thoughts I might have had got tossed in the Atlantic before I reached home. When I got in the cottage I went directly to the phone and placed a call to Steve Moore. I told him I had a problem. I could hear the groan clearly.

"Steve, listen to me, please." I told him the whole story.

When I finished, he said, "Dianne's niece? Fifteen you said?"

"Yeah. He's got to be near thirty. A real piece of work."

"Honeymoon, huh. If they're holed up there, we've probably been watching them anyhow. What room?"

"Second floor front, 210."

"What'd you say his name is?"

"Jingles, Jangles, some goddamn thing. I'm not sure."

"That's good enough. Someone down here probably knows him."

"There's pills under some towels in the bathroom. Enough for possession with intent to sell."

"Anything else?"

"Yeah, there is. Tell them to go in easy. I don't think the guy's got any weapons. I'm sure if he'd had any, he wouldn't have let me out of that rattrap with the fifty bucks."

"Okay. That makes a big difference." Steve hesitated, then added, "I figure this is the first call you ever made like this, huh? Don't let it bother you. She's not going to get hurt. And you didn't have a choice."

No matter what Steve had said, I knew I did have a choice and it did bother me. That night I drank a six-pack of Heineken and popped the last two Xanax. I passed out with my clothes on.

Epilogue

"HAVE YOU SEEN your kids lately, Dan?" Steve Moore asked.

It was just after six o'clock. Steve had called me earlier, said he wanted to talk. I figured it was about the Honeymoon Hotel incident. We were both in jeans and T-shirts sitting on the railing with our backs to the beach. Straight across from us, on the far side of Ocean Boulevard, was the Funland Arcade. It was the middle of June, about two weeks since Ted Norris had been killed in my cottage. My arm was still bandaged from the bullet I'd taken, but wasn't as painful as before. I didn't feel too bad overall, either. In fact, I felt pretty good with the wind blowing off the ocean against my back and a couple of painkillers in my bloodstream.

"I see them once a month. That's all the court'll let me."

"That's bullshit," Steve said. "Those are your kids too. You've got a right to see them more than that."

"I know. But I don't have the stomach to fight it after all that's gone down. Besides, maybe they're right. Maybe it's better for the kids not to see me more, not just yet anyway." Steve didn't say anything for a bit. I sat there, holding tight to the railing.

Finally he said, "If there's anything I can do, you know, go to court, character reference...anything."

"I know, Steve, thanks." I wanted to change the subject. "How's Kelsey doing?" Kelsey had been staying with Steve and his wife since the incident at my cottage.

Steve lit up. "He's doing good. I got him a job."

"Oh, yeah. Where?"

"He's gonna be a dishwasher at the White Cap for the summer."

"That'll be good for him."

"Sure it will. Keep him out of trouble and give him some spending money. Maybe keep his mind busy and not on what's happened recently." Steve hesitated, spoke again. "Although we've taken him to his mother's grave."

"How did that go?"

"He was a brave soldier."

I didn't know what to say to that.

People strolled by and Steve and I watched them pass. We must've looked like two seagulls perched up on the railing. Only our eyes moved and we didn't speak for a while. It wasn't a summer crowd out yet, although it would be in another week or two. But it was June and the weather was nice. There were quite a few singles and couples walking by and groups of teenagers chattering away without a care in the world. I thought about how lucky they were. Two rollerbladers weaved in and out between the walkers, and across Ocean Boulevard I could hear the bells and whistles at the Funland Arcade.

"Dan?" Steve turned to look at me and I looked back. "Yeah?"

"The wife wants to adopt Kelsey. She's getting awfully fond of him." He hesitated, then smiled. "I guess I am too, for that matter."

I nodded. "What's there not to be fond of? He's a good boy. Cora raised him well."

"We're going to try and get permanent custody for now." Steve looked at me hard, as if maybe he wondered if I approved.

He didn't have to wonder. I did approve. Steve and his wife had no children. I didn't know why. They'd be good for Kelsey and he for them. "What about Ober Sweeney?"

Steve snorted. "He's going to do heavy time on the cookin' charges. Mona Freeman too. So he won't be in the picture. He doesn't want anything to do with the boy anyway. The only other relatives Kelsey has aren't much better. I don't think there's anyone that can or will object."

"How do you think he's taking it all?"

Steve shook his head in what looked like amazement. "Considering what he's been through, he's doing great."

"That's 'cause he's a great kid."   And for a moment I felt a little jealous of Steve and his wife and wondered why I hadn't let the boy live with me.   Then I remembered — I already had a family and I wanted a normal relationship with them again.   More than anything.

And somehow, when the time was right, I knew that would happen. So the best place I could imagine Kelsey ending up was with Steve and his wife. I took a deep breath, relieved knowing Kelsey was finally going to be okay. They'd all be good for each other. I didn't have any doubt about that.

I took another deep breath, filling my head with the sea air and the aroma of fried dough, something I've never tried if you can believe it.   "What's going to happen to Beautiful Beach Real Estate?"

"The feds seized it. They'll probably be selling it. Want to get into the real estate business?"

"I'd rather get eaten by a shark." I heard the clickety-clack of a skateboard and spun my head, half-expecting to see my son or Kelsey. A younger girl, probably not ten, was headed our way. She wore a helmet, something I knew neither of the boys would be caught dead in outside of maybe a competition. She glided by with a competent air.

"What about the rest of them?"

Steve chuckled.   "Lenny Quarters and Frankie Earring? Those two hard-ons? We're working on it. We're pretty sure Quarters was distributing Norris's meth to his Massachusetts connections. Hopefully, the feds'll put him away on that. Frankie Earring? He'll probably get a parole violation on the B&E's and hot goods. And even if they don't get locked up this time around, we'll have other shots at them down the road, knowing those two."

"I suppose you will. The beach'd sure be better off without them." The thought of those two reminded me of something. "Why the hell did they try to set up Kelsey to get caught breaking into Lenny Quarter's arcade?"

"Norris was behind that. Just another one of his ideas to try and put pressure on Mrs. Sweeney to keep her mouth shut."

"Jesus, he tried everything except taking her out to dinner."

"Too much of a tight wad for that." Steve shifted on the railing. "What about Kelly and the other guy? And Dianne? How are they doing?"

"Shamrock? He's back to work. Hobbling around but otherwise good as new. Guillermo and Dianne are both good too."

"They're all real lucky. It could've turned out a lot worse. Especially for you."

A small shudder ran through me. "We were lucky, weren't we?"

Steve must've heard my voice crack because he quickly changed the subject. "You heard about how that ended up?" He pointed in the direction of the Honeymoon Hotel."

I nodded. "I read about the raid in the *Union*. Dianne told me the rest."

"At least she doesn't have to worry about her niece spending time with Jingles anymore. We got him on the 'with intent' charge, plus he was on probation. He'll do at least a couple of years."

"I thought it was Jangles?"

"It's shit now." We both laughed.

"Dianne's gotten Crystal into a good rehab," I said. "She's keeping her fingers crossed."

"That's all you can do."

"You think with Norris's death the hard drugs might die down a little?" I asked even though I already knew the answer.

"You and I been around too long to think that, Dan. Matter of fact, we're already watching someone else. Want to hear about it?"

"No thanks."

Steve laughed. "I couldn't tell you anyhow."

"Good."

Steve cleared his throat. "She's a nice woman...Dianne."

"She is." We were both silent. I could tell Steve was waiting for me to continue. I didn't.

Finally he said, "So what are you going to do now?"

I knew he didn't mean tonight, even though he probably expected me to answer that way. "Try and get my life back together." And I meant it.

I could tell by the look on his face that I was right about what he'd expected. He seemed uncomfortable. "You will. I know you will. And like I said, if there's anything I can do, well..." He turned away, took a breath.

"Thanks, Steve." There was an awkward minute of silence.

"Well, I gotta get going," Steve said as he hopped off the railing. "I promised Kelsey some Wally's pizza tonight. I'm looking forward to it."

Steve stuck out his hand; I shook it. His hand was dry, mine wasn't. "Yeah, sure, Steve. I'll see you around the beach. I'm not going anywhere."

"Okay." He turned to go, hesitated, turned back. "And...ahh...you know, anytime you want to visit Kelsey, you know where we live. Don't be a stranger. It's a small beach after all."

"That's for sure. Thanks and tell Kelsey I said hi."

He headed over to an unmarked police car parked in one of the spots facing the ocean. The red parking violation flag was up. I smiled. Steve hopped in the car, backed out of the spot, and drove off up Ocean Boulevard.

The sky was getting dark and so were my thoughts. A dangerous combination for someone like me. Off in the distance I heard the cackle of the shooting gallery mannequins. Then I remembered—Shamrock was off tonight. He'd be drinking at the Crooked Shillelagh. Thank god I had him and one pain-free arm to lift beer. I slid off the railing and headed in the direction I'd gone a thousand nights before. A direction that felt like it led nowhere now. But that wouldn't last forever. Someday my life would fall back into place. I knew it would. It had to. I'd make it.

Until then I had to hang on to the one thing I had left—Hampton Beach.

About the Author

Jed Power is a Hampton Beach, NH-based writer and author of numerous published short stories. *The Boss of Hampton Beach* was his first novel in the Dan Marlowe crime series.

Watch for *Blood on Hampton Beach*, the third novel in the Dan Marlowe series. Coming Soon.

Find out more at www.darkjettypublishing.com.

Made in the USA
Middletown, DE
11 November 2016